of

THE KINGS OF PENDAR

The Ghosts of Pendar

TROY A. SKOG

Copyright © 2020 Troy A. Skog

Cover Art: Elle Arden

Editor: Heather Savage,

Staccato Publishing

All rights reserved.

Printed in USA

ISBN: 9798691735912

To all those that have gone before, until we meet again.

Books by Troy A. Skog

The Kings of Pendar Series:

The Remnants

Jewel of the Elves

The Trolls of Blackwater Deep

The Orphan's Revenge

The Dragon Spell

The Ghosts of Pendar

****

2021 Into the Darkness

Welcome to Pendar!

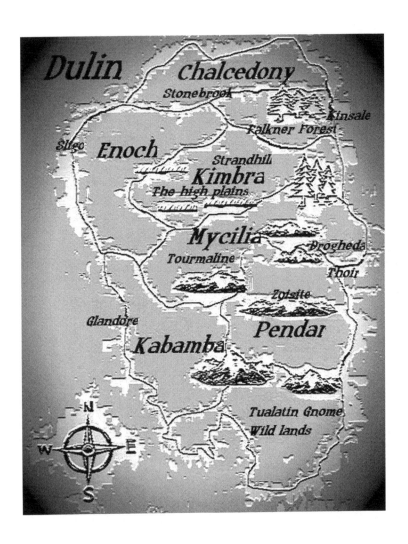

PROLOGUE

The arrows, tipped with dwarven steel, burned painfully as they easily pierced his thickening dragon skin in quick succession. For a moment the arrows felt as if his own dragon's fire had been injected inside the wounds to burn him to his very core. Then, as soon as the pain became unbearable, it evaporated away as he took a long ragged halting breath and collapsed to the ground.

Struggling to free himself from an invisible entanglement, he finally climbed to his feet and the world seemed to swirl about him. His first instinct was to finish the transformation to the dragon and escape from those who were swarming. He spoke the dragon spell again, just as he had before those deadly missiles came streaking at him, except now the dragon didn't respond to his call.

The dwarves seemed to pay no attention to him, though maybe they too struggled to see him in the haze suddenly muting the landscape around them. He thought to use it to his advantage. In desperation he turned, looking for a path to run away from the growing crowd.

Darting about, he tried to avoid running into them though he quickly realized that it didn't matter if he did. Turning to squeeze through small gaps he floated with ease between the broad dwarves who gathered, now staring down at the ground. Their interest sparked his curiosity and his eyes followed theirs as he paused to look back. There on the ground lay a familiar form, one that looked much like his own.

The words came blurting out before he could stop himself and he rushed back to the fallen's side, dropping to his knees. The truth of the situation hammered home in that moment. "No, this isn't how it's supposed to end."

"Come now Rathlin, there will be time to lament this failure later. Where is the book of spells you stole from my castle? Focus, I need you to insert this spell into the book before you are too far from the living. Quickly now."

Rathlin took the spell from Dungarvan and did as he was bid, inserting the sheet that contained the spell within the pages of the book before returning to his father's side.

"I know there are many questions swirling through your mind right now. The most important one is that this is only temporary. Death won't keep us in its icy grip forever. Now we go to the mountain to wait."

CHAPTER ONE

"You've done a great job getting everyone settled into Drogheda. I couldn't have done all this without you at my side."

"It's been my pleasure, Your Highness. My staff, along with myself, are at your disposal day or night."

"Speaking of that," Samuel paused in shuffling the papers spread across the entire surface of his desk to look up at Mayor Tralee, "how long will it take to get used to living in the mountain? I wake up in, what I think is the morning, and then emerge from my rooms to find the rest of the city still asleep."

"It's only been a little over a month, mayhap two since you arrived." He looked up over his spectacles from his own pile of papers he had been reading. "You will get used to living within the mountain, though I would recommend you step outside daily to feel the sun on your skin."

"Thanks, I will keep that in mind. In fact, maybe now would be a good time?"

The mayor paused in his reading, taking the hint that the king was looking for a break from reviewing reports. Straightening up the pile he had spread before himself, he worked quickly to take his leave.

"We can take these up again tomorrow, I think we covered the most urgent concerns."

"You are most correct, Your Highness." Mayor Tralee nodded before he stood and bowed to Samuel, spun, and scurried from the room.

Samuel felt bad about dismissing his faithful servant for just a moment before remembering his father struggling with the dullness of overseeing an entire kingdom from the chair in his private offices. Grinning to himself, he realized his father had gotten the last laugh. He was off living in a cabin in the woods while Samuel sat and read the endless reports on everything from food supplies to steel wares being shipped from the docks of Thoir.

Though he felt remorse for sending the mayor on his way, it didn't cross his mind to call after him to get him to return once he was beyond the door. Realizing he may have actually just stolen a few moments to himself he stood and stretched his legs before he moved out from behind his desk to pace across the room to the cabinet that held a few of his personal effects. Anxious to look at one in particular that he had stashed away, but had not had the time to peruse up until this moment.

Pulling the door open he looked within, his eyes passing over all else to settle on the one that drew his attention. Rathlin's bag. Reaching in he pulled it out and carried it over to the table that sat off to the side of his desk. Holding it up and looking at it from all angles, he spun it about before setting it down on the time worn wood table.

Standing back, he stared at it for long moments, considering the path it had traveled to finally land in his office to be tucked away within his cabinet. With the death of Rathlin and the defeat of his army the tent that held his few belongings had been searched and, once deemed safe to handle, cataloged and sent within the mountain to be reviewed, and possibly researched at a later date.

The sudden departure of his father Edward, and subsequent coronation of Samuel, had everyone scrambling within the mountain, the bag had been left behind and forgotten. Samuel discovered it during the inspection of his new quarters, deciding to keep it quiet, but until now had not had time to inspect the contents. Taking a moment to push aside the mounds of papers on his desk, he repositioned the pack on the smooth wooden surface.

Reaching out he loosened the straps and hesitantly poured the contents out onto the table, tossing the bag aside as his eyes were drawn to one item in particular; a thick old leather tome that had fallen open to reveal writings within. Daring not to touch it, he leaned in, inspecting the precise, measured handwriting on the weathered pages. It took Samuel no time at all before he figured out what he had before him, Rathlin's book of spells.

There was rumor of its existence in the items retrieved from Rathlin's tent, though the oversight of allowing it to be lost and lay unprotected within his cupboard was deserving of a reprimand, but not at this very moment. Not before he had a chance to look through its contents.

Tentatively reaching out, he touched the worn paper before quickly yanking his hand back in case he had triggered a trap laid upon it by its previous possessor. The book did not move of its own volition and no swirling cloud of poisonous fumes burst forth, rather it laid unassuming upon the smooth wooden table. Growing bolder, Samuel once again reached out to feel the pages beneath his fingers, forcing himself to maintain the contact as if to prove to himself that it was safe and could do him no harm.

The paper was soft beneath his fingers as he let them glide over the surface, careful not to touch the writings upon them for fear that he would smudge them. Bending over he looked at the text he was subconsciously protecting for the first time.

Whomever had written the words upon the page had been a practiced hand. When he was a student his teacher, Master Gosford, would have been pleased if Samuel had ever achieved anything close to this level of quality in his writing lessons. He wished now that he had paid more attention when Master Gosford spoke of different languages as he couldn't read a word of what was written so beautifully upon the creamy pages.

Braver now that he hadn't been turned into a frog to hop about the room, he began to turn the pages. He was unsure yet what he was looking for as the pages flipped one after another until at last he stopped. Unsure at first, he did a double take as if his eyes were deceiving him. The letters on this page alone moved and shuffled until they realigned themselves in the common tongue. That alone should have cried out to him as a warning, but instead drew him in even more assuredly.

Without his previous caution, he began to read aloud the words written in the same skilled hand.

Mist of the Mountain

The path lay before the stricken, the weight of the mountain pressing down on he who walked alone on his final journey with his sword at his back. The air swirled about his legs as he passed through the world around him. The haze before his eyes served as a distraction to conceal the truth of his purpose.

Samuel paused in his reading, the air about him becoming the very haze the writing spoke of as he looked around the room. His heart quickened at the realization of what was happening. Looking back at the book, the letters once again took flight across the page and scrambled back into the mysterious language. He struggled to draw breath as the spell wove itself around him. Staggering as the mist grew thick, he reached for anything to steady himself. Finding only the wizard's pack, he gripped it fruitlessly. Samuel choked on the wizard's spell as it expanded to fill the room with its suffocating mist, before falling unconscious in a heap, scattering the book and the contents of the bag.

Coughing violently Samuel came awake. Pushing himself up, he paused in his efforts as he pressed a hand to his pounding head. He wasn't sure how much time had passed, but his mouth was dry. With his thirst driving him he headed for the door, not looking back, but pausing as he felt the urge to grab his magical sword that hung by the door. Strapping it across his back, the familiar weight momentarily reassured him.

Outside the room he stopped in the hall. Turning he looked at the closed door, his memory foggy as to whether he opened the door before walking through. Attributing it to the haze that hung at the periphery of his mind he put it aside and went in search of the liquid his throat demanded to quench his thirst.

The hallway was empty, a curiosity at this time of day, though he brushed it aside unsure exactly how long he had laid on the floor. For all he knew it could be the middle of the night by now. He shook his head remembering the mayor's assertion that he would come to know the movement of the sun above the longer he lived within the mountain. Turning down a side hall he stopped, considering the distant sounds of the Ballaghaderreen falls.

His thirst spoke to him and he changed his intended path to the dining room, heading for the great falls that carried water through the heart of the mountain. The desire to quench his thirst guided his steps as he walked the empty hallways of Drogheda, even though drinking directly from the falls was an impossibility.

The rush of the falls grew louder the closer he got until at last he emerged on the Galway bridge that spanned the cavern. Stepping out of the cavern he looked upon the heroes of Drogheda who lined the bridge, eyes following the bigger than life statues until they landed on a pair of cloaked figures standing upon the bridge and watching the falls.

The curiosity of finally seeing another person, much less two, within the mountain overrode any caution he should have exhibited. He closed the distance between them, neither of the mysterious figures turning to look his way even as Samuel came to stand next to them. For long moments the pair stood in silence looking upon the falls. When at long last one of them spoke the sound of his voice startled Samuel from his reverie, the voice oddly familiar.

"I thought you would never come. I have waited for too many years. What is your name?"

"My name is Samuel, I'm the king of Pendar, I mean Drogheda."

"You have ascended to the throne, I see. I knew your father, and mother, for that matter."

"Are you as thirsty as I am?"

"I am. That's how I knew you would come here, but we need to go now. I see you have brought the sword as I instructed. It's good to know you follow instructions."

"Is your friend coming?" Samuel nodded to the other standing to the far side of the cloaked figure.

"He is my son, you may know him."

Samuel looked through the haze at the other man, but no recollection came to him. The leader of the pair turned and walked away deeper into the mountain. Though he didn't know why Samuel followed his lead, the other following protectively behind them. A chorus of hammers at work on stone ahead of him comforted his muted senses.

Mayor Tralee knocked on the door to Samuel's office, waiting several moments before announcing himself as he pushed the door open a crack. "Your Highness, I didn't see you in the dining hall so I assumed you were here."

Getting no response he stepped in an looked about the office. A torch on the wall still flickered, though it had burned low and gave off minimal light. He scanned for a spare before going to the cabinet to get another to light even though the king wasn't visible. Stepping around the desk he nearly tripped over the body of Samuel whose body laid prostrate on the floor behind the desk.

"Samuel, are you okay?" he asked as he knelt down and gently nudged the young king. "Samuel?" His voice rose as the man laying on the floor made no response. Putting his ear to his chest he checked to make sure the heart still beat within. It was low but steady, yet the king would not wake at his prodding. The mayor knew not what ailed the king, and fought to push down the anxiety that threatened to cause his own heart to burst from his chest. Knowing he needed help, the old dwarf hustled from the room looking for a healer to bring the king back from his mysterious slumber.

CHAPTER TWO

They left the bridge through the tunnel opposite the one he had come through to look upon the falls. The trio left the falls behind along with the rush of the water. The sound of hammers striking chisels floated up to them on the air as they entered the tunnels, louder in the confines of the dwarven hewn passageways now that the falls were growing more distant.

Samuel didn't ask any more questions after they left the falls, at least for quite some time. Instead he tried to focus on his surroundings though the harder he tried, the more frustrated he became. The flames from the torches seemed to flicker with their usual intensity, but the light was washed away in the haze that seemed to affect the pathways further down in the mountain as much as it did by the falls. It was some time later he realized that even when there were no torches throwing off light he didn't need them to see in the dark. Panic threatened to wash over him and he quickly spoke up.

"Excuse me, can you see in the darkness too?"

"The torches we carry provide the light." The man ahead of him responded over his shoulder

"What torches?" Samuel asked as suddenly the man in the lead turned to show him the one that he carried and pointed to the one that Samuel now found in his hand.

"Please, no more questions. We have far to travel."

Samuel obeyed. The man's tone offered no other option, though the surprise discovery of the torch in his own hand was just as effective at silencing him. Lifting the torch before him he stared at it for many long moments, fighting through the haze that covered his mind as he tried to remember whether the torch had been there all along. After much deliberation, and a glance over his shoulder at the man following him to see his, he couldn't refute the man's assertion. He must have been carrying it. Why couldn't he remember?

Time seemed to have no meaning as they went deeper into the mountain, coursing through the tunnels that the long lived dwarves had constructed many, many generations ago. With every mile they walked the sound of the chisels working the stone grew closer, yet remained distant at the same time. The anticipation of finally meeting the dwarves Samuel knew to be working ahead of them drew him ever forward and helped to keep his mind off the thirst that never seemed to relent, until it didn't.

His throat was so dry he decided he would have to break the silence the trio had maintained for many hours even if it again brought scorn from the man who led them. "By chance do you have a canteen?" His hope was that the man would produce one as he had the torch earlier, though this time he was soon to be disappointed.

"There will be a time for that, but we have far to travel before then."

"How far are we going today before we stop to rest and eat?" Samuel felt diminished and could only attribute it to the fact that though they had walked what must be many miles they had never stopped for a meal.

"Again, just as with the water, we will eat only when we have reached our destination. I beg of you no more questions while we are within the mountain. It would be a shame to garner unwanted attention."

"From who?" Samuel couldn't stop himself in time and received a sinister glare from his guide.

"Too late."

Voices ahead in the tunnel had Samuel peeking around the cloaked man to see a squad of dwarves emerging from the haze and striding purposefully in his direction. With their hammers in hand they marched forward to stop in front of the trio. Samuel blinked, trying to decide if it was just more of the haze or if the dwarves weren't covered in dirt, head to toe. Their leader stepped out and began to question them interrupting his ongoing inspection.

"I thought we told you to get out of Drogheda. Who are these other two and how did they get into the mountain?"

"I'm King Samuel Ellingstone." Samuel stepped out to address one of his subjects.

"I don't care much that you're a king up on the surface. Within these halls you are not but an intruder."

"Excuse me master dwarf, I beg your pardon. Mayhap you have been down in the tunnels mining for some time, but I have indeed been elevated to take the throne from my father Edward Ellingstone."

Questioning stares were all that greeted him from the squad of dwarves as they became restless behind their spokesman.

"Surely you have heard of my father, King Edward of Pendar, and with him stepping down after the destruction of Pendar I am now King of Drogheda."

Shouts from the dwarves replaced the silence that had fallen over the tunnel caused Samuel to step back from their clear anger.

"We need to be going, now." The tall cloaked man stated as he gripped Samuel's shoulder. The sight of the angry squad of dwarves only reinforced the declaration and Samuel willingly let the man guide his steps as they turned and raced away from the mob close on their heels.

Struggling to keep up with the cloaked figures Samuel leaned forward and pumped his legs as fast as he could get them to go. The speed which the men ran compared to the dwarves had the trio outdistancing the squad before too long, though the men didn't stop to rest even after the sounds of pursuit died away. It was only after they had run nearly a quarter of the way back to the falls did the man in charge stop.

"What was all that about?" Samuel got out between coughs, his throat seemingly even more dry from the exertion. "They didn't recognize me as their king, and indeed threatened me. I need to get back to the hall and speak with General Halfthor immediately."

"I would caution you against going back. Obviously not everything is as it seems in Drogheda."

"Exactly, that's why we need to talk to Relysis."

"To me, it appears the dwarves are not so accepting of you, a human, taking the dwarven throne as your own."

"They cheered at my coronation ceremony. The dwarves love the Ellingstone family." Samuel's voice was rising and the tall man held up a hand to ask him to quiet his voice. "This is ridiculous," Samuel finished trailing off to a low whisper.

"We will get to the bottom of it, but I think we need to keep moving. I know a trail that we can take to get around these dissidents." The tall man didn't stop and wait for Samuel to agree, instead he began to walk off, leading them down an alternate route that bisected their own.

Samuel fell in line with minimal prodding from the silent one, he was still rattled by the dwarves who denied his claim to the throne. They had openly challenged him and sought to seize him, or worse. This revelation only deepened the haze around him, no longer at his periphery. He allowed it pull him down deeper into its clutches.

CHAPTER THREE

The mayor sat in silence with the other members in the council room as Willos entered with his assistant Birr close behind him. Mayor Tralee could see clearly as he looked upon Willos that he was prepared to make some hard decisions if it were required.

"The news has surely reached all ears within the city and even the village outside the gate. I guess there was no stopping it, but I would have rather had an answer to what ails the king travel along with that news. Mayor, what can you tell us? Have there been any changes today, any difference to the king's health since he was found collapsed a week past?"

"I've checked on him several times a day, as I know a few of you have also." The mayor nodded to Willos and Birr as he had come upon them both separately and together at the side of the king. "However, for those who don't have time from your duties to stop in, there has been no change in his health. His heart beats slowly within his chest, barely detectable at times, and his breathing is nothing more than a whisper."

"Has any explanation been offered as to what has afflicted him? Is there a danger to anyone else within the city?" A gruff voice from the back of the room questioned.

Mayor Tralee didn't see the questioner, so he addressed the group as a whole. "No one other than Samuel has fallen ill."

"Was it poison?"

The question startled the mayor, the mere thought that someone within Drogheda would threaten the king's life seemed unfathomable. "It was not considered as far as I know." Turning to Willos for guidance the High Council took over the discussion.

"There were measures taken to determine if that occurred, however, none of the dwarves who sampled the king's food were stricken with the same illness."

The mayor nearly toppled over at Willos' statement. He had not known of that part of the investigation. His mind raced, concerned now at the thought that Willos may have suspected him of trying to assassinate the king and had shielded him from knowing. Willos' apologetic eyes confirmed for him that the councilman had done what he needed to do in the moment and it was not personal, though the mayor was still indignant.

"I could have told you that I hadn't tampered with the king's meal, if you had asked. There was no need to risk the lives of those dwarves in case the poison had come from someone else."

"We still had to know, and now that we know there isn't an imminent threat I think it's time to send a runner to retrieve Isabel. She is next in line to the throne and the sooner she is back, the better."

The mayor turned inward for much of the rest of the meeting. They had no right to even consider that he would harm the king, the two of them worked impossibly well together in his estimation at running the city. He even dared consider the young king a friend. Snapped from his musings as the meeting adjourned he headed for the door along with the members of the council and had almost made it out of the chamber when Willos called out to him.

"Yes, how can I assist the High Council?"

"Come now Tralee, I didn't mean anything by keeping you from knowing about the investigation into the poisoning, or thankfully not, of the king's meal."

"Have I not been helpful in answering every manner of question that has been posed to me?"

"Of course. Your knowledge of the king's daily habits has been invaluable, if not eye opening, at the amount of time you have spent with him."

"I'm just trying to help him understand the workings of Drogheda. It's not as easy as some would suspect."

"Those words have never crossed my lips."

"You are forgiven Willos, but I do have much to do, are there any more questions?"

"Just one. Can you recall any other time Samuel has taken Rathlin's bag of belongings out of storage? We were wondering if someone had come to try and retrieve it."

"I had not seen it out in his chambers before. It's the only thing that was out of place in his office and has since been returned to its place. Are you looking into that too?"

"We have looked over the contents, but have discovered nothing sinister with the items that were spilled, even the book of spells itself is in an unknown language so they could not even be read by accident."

"I will keep reviewing the time surrounding the incident and see if I can remember anything else that may have escaped my memory." Taking his leave from Willos the mayor coursed his way through the tunnels until he arrived at the hospital.

"How is the king doing today? Have there been any sign of improvement?" Mayor Tralee asked as he entered the hospital ward within Drogheda.

"Sorry Mayor, he has laid here in his bed without barely any sign of life for the entire day."

"I think I'll sit with him for just a while, if that is okay." The mayor knew without asking that it was fine with the healers that he sit with him just as he had every day for the past week. As he pulled his chair over to his customary position he was startled to hear mumbling from behind him. Letting go of the chair he spun and looked expectantly at Samuel.

"Did you hear that?" Tralee nearly yelled at the healer who was already coming towards the bed, before turning back to the king. "Samuel? Are you awake?"

"I did, though I don't know what he said."

Samuel interrupted the pair as they spoke to one another, his ramblings unintelligible but for a few words as he suddenly thrashed about before becoming once again both still and silent.

"Send an assistant to get Willos, I need to go check on something." Tralee didn't wait for the healer's response, instead he bolted from the room and moved as quickly as he could on rickety knees that hadn't paced faster than a quick walk in decades.

Arriving at Samuel's quarters he rushed past the posted guard who, recognizing the king's hand, did not step forward to dissuade him, and threw open the door and scanned the office for what he knew must be missing. The king's magical sword was gone from where it always hung when it wasn't strapped to the king's back. He couldn't believe he had missed it up until now, however, the reason he remembered it was even more perplexing. Samuel, in his mysterious sleep had just spoken of needing it, and if Tralee had heard him correctly, to battle dwarves.

CHAPTER FOUR

"Why are you stopping? We need to keep moving if we are going to reach the Western door before I start to gather dirt in my own beard. I've waited a long time in this mountain and I'm ready to get out from under the weight."

"Have you crossed paths with the dwarves before?" Samuel asked as he sat down and adjusted the sword hanging at his back.

"You saw their confusion upon seeing you. Clearly they have spent too much time in the depths of the mountain."

Samuel caught the quick nod from the tall man directed over his shoulder at the silent one, spinning his head he was momentarily sure that there was a quick gesture given in return. Though the wave of confusion that washed over him in that moment had him doubting what his eyes had seen. He shook his head at the haze that seemed to surround him.

"Alright, that's settled then. Let's get moving."

Samuel got back to his feet and followed the tall one's instruction knowing the quiet one would be quick to reinforce his orders. Adjusting his belt he slid his fingers, absently searching for a canteen that didn't exist. In all his life he couldn't remember being so thirsty.

The trio walked for untold hours without any more breaks, the tall one pushing the pace and dissuading any conversation by ignoring any question put forth by Samuel. Samuel had eventually gotten the message that there would be no response to any of his queries and instead focused on the tunnels they passed through.

Even through his haze there were many marvelous sights to behold. The dwarves of old had spent many long hours carving the likeness of their heroes and legends into the rock columns and reliefs that lined the walkways. It was while he was looking upon one grouping in particular that he stopped and stared. The silent one tried to push him forward though only partially succeeded as Samuel braced himself.

"These dwarves in this carving, they look like the ones who confronted us earlier."

"That's unlikely. Your mind is playing tricks on you. We've been below ground for too long." The leader of the trio stated, turning to look at the others behind him.

"No, I'm not, and look at this. The plaque right here states that they were all killed in a mining accident." Samuel's voice trailed off, his mind fighting to make sense of what he had just read. A flicker of movement from the silent one preceded another wave of confusion much like the last one, though this one staggered him visibly and he struggled to remain upright. The firm grip on his arm from the tall cloaked figure kept him on his feet, though the pain he felt was harder to hold at bay.

"We've not the time to discuss this here and now. Move."

Samuel stumbled a few steps until his world stopped pitching back and forth and he shook free of the fingers digging into his arm. The silent one behind him pushed him forward, again it was less a request than demand. With his head still swirling he gave way and heeded the instruction, his focus on not throwing up until the nausea faded.

Drawing inward Samuel sought to protect himself, though from what he couldn't put his finger on. The cloaked men always knew best and continued to guide him through the tunnels with a knowledge that he himself as the king of Drogheda seemed to lack.

In a moment of clarity he pushed himself to make a mental note to remedy this shortcoming once he returned back from the outskirts to the city proper and got a proper escort, armed escort he added, to tour the labyrinth of tunnels that comprised Drogheda.

The thought that he would need a detail of guards to walk the tunnels in safety struck him as odd. The dwarves hadn't known him at all and felt threatened by his, no, their presence. Why? That was all the further he was able to explore that thought when shouts from ahead froze the trio in their tracks.

"It's the dwarves again," the tall cloaked figure hissed over his shoulder.

The dwarves had their hammers out and were barreling towards them in a wedge formation. They appeared determined to rid their halls of the perceived interlopers and, unlike last time, there was not going to be any time for discussion. With the threat closing the gap between them Samuel instinctively reached for his sword.

"Not in here!" shouted the tall one as he grabbed Samuel's arm. "That magical sword won't do you any good and you'll have every dwarf in the mountain, living and dead, chasing us."

Samuel didn't have any time to argue as he was shoved backwards by the tall one, simultaneously shouting instructions at the silent one. "You make yourself useful and take care of these dwarves. I don't intend to be chased through these tunnels forever."

There was naught but a nod in response. Samuel was pushed further away and past the silent one who seemed to be growing in size beneath his cloak. Alarm bells rang through the haze that lay over his mind as he tried to make sense of it. Just as they ducked around a corner a bright blue ball of flame lit up the tunnel behind them. Screams from the dwarves echoed off the rock until the roar of the flames replaced them.

Samuel tried to put the puzzle pieces together as he stood pinned against the wall, the cold breath of the cloaked figure washing over his face as they waited for whatever had transpired in the adjacent hall to come to an end. Long moments passed after the screams and flame. The silent one broke the uneasy quiet when he called out that the way was all clear.

Strong hands pushed him forward. The leader of the trio apparently had none of the trepidation Samuel felt. The silent one stood, smoke swirling around him, in the center of the tunnel. His cloak no longer swollen, he wore a satisfied smile. It was the first such expression Samuel had seen from within the shadows of the hood.

"Quickly now, we don't have much time until the alarms start to sound within this crypt."

Samuel was pushed ahead once again at the leader's announcement. Still unsure of what had just happened within the tunnel, there was no sign of the pack of angry dwarves, he willingly followed in the man's wake. Time seemed to have no meaning now as they trod the maze of passages the dwarves had carved through the mountain.

Though unsure if he could keep going he forced himself to follow their leader through every twist and turn, fearful of the power exhibited by the man who walked behind him. He had quickly disposed of the rushing pack of dwarves single handedly in the blink of an eye, and with an unearthly blue flame. There was more to him than he appeared, he was one Samuel dared not cross until he had could learn more. Samuel was pulled from his thoughts when suddenly the tall one slowed his pace to a walk and entered a small room where he stopped. A short, wizened figure barred their way to exit through door on the far side.

"So your wait was finally rewarded. I was beginning to think this plan of yours was never going to come to pass."

"You have grown bold since your death, Kropett. Be careful, there are worse things than being a ghost."

"So you have brought an extra guest," the diminutive gnome stated somewhat soberly.

"Samuel you have never met, though it was by mere moments that you missed his birth. The other you may remember from his studies, my son Rathlin."

"Indeed I do, Master Dungarvan, indeed I do."

CHAPTER FIVE

"How can his sword be missing?" Relysis growled, his eyes scanning the king's chambers as if it would somehow miraculously appear.

Relysis' ire wasn't directed at anyone, but Mayor Tralee felt as if he himself stood accused of secreting the sword from the king's chamber. "I'm not sure when I saw it last, it wasn't my main concern when I found Samuel sprawled unconscious on the floor. The theft, if that's what you're calling it, could have happened at any time after he was moved to the healers."

"Or it could have happened at the time he was struck down." Willos suggested an alternative option. "There were guards posted at the door within moments of the discovery, and have been ever since, so it seems to me that's when someone seized the opportunity."

"He spoke of battling dwarves."

"Samuel said what? When was this?" Willos asked.

"In the hospital ward. It was nearly incoherent and he was still unconscious. That's why I came down here looking for it and then immediately sought out you and the general."

"What dwarves would be plotting against the king? None within the army of Pendar, I can assure you."

"Pendar was different Relysis, it was a city that blended the two races. Could there be a faction within the mountain that resents a human sitting upon the throne of Drogheda?"

"Bah, I won't believe it. Samuel is forged from the same material as his father, and grandfather before him."

"I too would rather not believe it, but you've spent a lot of years by the side of the king's father and grandfather. Could it be that your perspective might be clouded by your close association."

"I agree with Relysis. I've never heard an ill word spoken against Samuel, or any of his family for that matter. Besides, Samuel was born within these halls. Human or not, he is one of us."

"I hear both of your arguments, however, we have no other leads than the rambling from a king in the throes of an unnatural sleep. Be discreet, but ask around. See if there are any whispers that bear further investigation."

The three dwarves sat in silence for many long moments as they each pondered the chances of a coordinated effort to harm the new king of Drogheda. With no immediate answers, Willos, followed by Relysis, took their leave.

Tralee, alone now in the king's chamber, took a moment to try and remember if anything else was amiss. He began to walk around the room. Coming around the corner of the desk his head swirled and he reached out to steady himself, pausing for just a moment as he remembered finding the stricken king lying on the floor. Waiting for his legs to steady, he continued the circuit he had begun with such high hopes of discovering something that had been missed.

The wizard's book of spells had been returned to the pack. He knew it was, by its very nature dangerous, though he felt that it might have helped in the investigation if the room had been left as it was at the time of the incident. Incident, he liked that word better than those he had heard in the High Council meeting. It sounded better to him that way. He definitely didn't want to call it an attack, or worse, an assassination attempt, and for sure didn't want to have his name associated with any such talk.

Pushing that thought away he returned to the back of the desk, unconsciously gripping the edge to prevent another dizzy spell. Excusing himself of the act of disrespecting the king he sat himself in Samuel's chair and surveyed the view from the king's perspective.

Stacks of papers lying undisturbed on the edges of the desk dispelled the idea that there had been a struggle anywhere near the desk.

"Ah," the word slipped past his lips. Willos had already discerned as much and that's why they had considered poisoning. "Still, you could have asked," he spoke aloud to the empty room.

It was in that moment he remembered there was something amiss with the desk. The papers were all stacked neatly in the corners. When he left the king alone that last time the desk was a mess from one end to the other. There hadn't been any organization to any of it, the young king didn't seem to have it in him no matter how many times he tried to instill the need for order into him.

He leaned back into the chair, reaching his hand up to stroke his beard. No one would clean up the desk after they struck down the king. Even if the papers had scattered in the struggle they would want to grab the sword and be off before anyone arrived to catch them in the act.

Tralee wasn't sure how this was important, but he knew it was a clue he could not easily brush aside. Pushing forward with that single focus he quickly concluded that Samuel had cleaned the surface of the desk intentionally and that meant that he wanted to give the wizard's bag of tricks his entire focus.

He knew where it had been placed and the mayor's eyes went to the closet that sat closed across the room. Standing, he walked across the room, tracing Samuel's steps in the path as he could only imagine. Pulling the door open he was immediately confronted by the very real fear of the thing he knew he needed to expose if he were to find the truth.

The pack was closed now, no longer open as it was that night, and its contents returned. Peering cautiously at it from all angles, he summoned the nerve to reach out and grasp the straps. Gritting his teeth he convinced himself that the pack itself couldn't possibly harm him and pushed aside his concern. Gripping the straps, he still almost expected some sort of jolt of magic as he pulled it free.

Carrying it carefully back to the table he continued to mimic as best as he could the probable steps that Samuel himself had taken. Pulling the pack open he quickly upended it and let the contents tumble out onto the table. He had no way to know how the items had been arranged when Samuel reviewed them, but Tralee had to wonder if the book of spells had come to rest at the center of the desk for the king too.

Tralee stood for long moments looking down at the book that seemed eager for him to reach out to touch it. That feeling alone gave him pause as he contemplated whether he should take the next step and open the cover. It reinforced his belief that the book was behind Samuel's affliction. Finally remembering that Willos had stated that the book was harmless, he tentatively reached out. Letting his fingers graze the leather, he tested whether Willos was correct before lifting the cover to explore what lay within.

Just as Willos suggested the book did not harm him, and too, the script was a language that Tralee didn't recognize, at least not at first. Carefully flipping the fragile pages he began to see words that were familiar. Sitting back in the chair he tried sifting through the studies of his youth. He had always appreciated the feel of a book in his hands to that of the handle of a battleaxe. Spending his youth learning mathematics and history instead of training with those that would become warriors in Pendar's army.

His natural inclinations had led him to a life of learning and it served him well becoming the mayor of Drogheda, though at the moment his focus was on deciphering the strange writings in the wizard's book of spells. Closing his eyes and diving deeper into memories of his lessons he sat in the quiet of the king's chambers for long moments that stretched to nearly an hour before his eyes popped open and an exclamation burst forth from his lips.

"Elvish!"

Standing up he leaned over the book and studied the writings once again. It was indeed elvish, but this was a version that was centuries old, if not older. Not even the elves of the Falkner forest still used this style in their standard missives between the two nations. The fact that they no longer wrote this way didn't deter Tralee, he knew how long lived the elves were even compared to dwarves. There could be someone within the elven forest who still knew the language and could solve the mystery of what was written within in the book of spells. He remembered that a runner had been sent to retrieve Isabel, but he wouldn't be sure Jade would come back with her to help in the translation.

With his excitement level rising he took a moment to flip a few more pages wanting to make sure he wasn't just imagining the similarity to ancient elvish. That old excitement and desire to learn drew him in as he flipped more pages until he arrived on a page where the script began to swirl and the letters arranged themselves so that he could read them easily.

The alarms in his mind began to ring in that very moment though he couldn't pull his eyes from the enchantment that had befallen him. The air about him filled with a mist and he blinked to clear his vision. Fighting the spell he now knew he had triggered he grabbed the tome in his hands and clutched it tight to his chest as he tried to run from the room.

Rounding the desk he pushed through the haze that filled the room, his focus on the door before him. His belief that if he could escape the room the cloud would be left behind him. Forcing his feet to keep moving he crept forward as if they were trapped in mud, the floor itself seeming to pull at him with every step. Gritting his teeth he pushed himself to fight the spell. Reaching for the handle his fingers fumbled as they tried to find a grip on the worn surface.

Scrambling, he nearly dropped the book he clutched to his chest as he fought to keep his feet under him. The haze about him grew thicker. His boots slid out from under him, his world going dark as he slumped to the floor.

Shaking his head to try to clear the cobwebs he climbed carefully to his feet. The haze refused to clear as he looked about the king's chamber, the memory of what had transpired creeping back to the forefront of his mind. It was then that he looked down at the prostrate form slumped over in front of the door still holding tight to the wizard's book and the mystery of what happened to the king became clear.

Pushing past the terror of seeing his own body lying propped against the door, not knowing if he was dead or alive, he gathered his courage. He knew that he alone understood the danger the book held, but now he too was lost in the haze as he assumed the king was. On the other hand he was the only one who might be able to reach the king in whatever world he now found himself and bring them both back.

Pulling the door open just enough to get his slightly rotund ethereal body through the door he could feel his inert form push the door closed behind him. Stepping into the hall he paused to see if the guard posted outside the door had registered anything that had happened within the room and that the mayor stood before him. The guard didn't move, not even as Tralee waved a hand in front of his face. With no response, Tralee bent an ear to listen for any sounds from the city. It was quiet for this time of day which seemed odd, however, distant hammers striking chisels called to him gently and with nothing else to guide him, he followed.

CHAPTER SIX

Relysis woke early that morning, his mind niggling on the mystery that surrounded the king's ailment and the missing sword. The magical sword's disappearance added a whole other layer to the situation, strongly suggesting the deep sleep that entrapped Samuel was not a coincidence nor an accident.

Swinging his feet over the edge of the bed he hopped down onto the cold granite floor, glad he slept with his wool socks on. After scurrying to find his britches he quickly tugged his boots on over his wool socks and found a sweater to pull on over his head. His pace slowed once he wrapped himself in some warmth, but didn't stoke the fire as he knew he would be soon out the door and heading back to the king's chamber to revisit it after he had a night to chew on it.

The halls were bustling with dwarves that were getting on with their tasks for the day, many heading for the dining hall before they went to the mines or out into the village outside the north gate to help rebuild from the battle with the dragon. Relysis ignored the rumblings in his own stomach as he coursed through the city on his way to the king's chambers.

"Good morning, General," the guard greeted Relysis with a quick salute as he neared the door.

"Has Mayor Tralee come by yet this morning?"

"I have been here all night and have not seen him, actually I was hoping you were my relief coming down the hall this morning."

"Then you'll be disappointed I didn't stop in the dining hall and bring you something to eat."

"Thank you for the thought General, but I came prepared." The guard pointed to the pack at his feet.

"Maybe I should be asking you for something to eat? No, I was just joking," Relysis added quickly as the guard began to reach for it. "I'll be fine, I just stopped by quick to look at something."

Grabbing the handle with his thick hands he gave the door a slight push and patted the guard on his wide shoulder. Stopping he looked at the door, his face bearing a puzzled expression.

"What is it, General?"

"I guess I shouldn't have skipped breakfast." He pushed again and the door resisted until Relysis, putting his shoulder into it, opened begrudgingly. It wasn't until the door was open enough for Relysis to see within did he realize there was someone lying on the floor behind the door. "Quick, help me here."

With the two of them working together they were able to push the door open wide enough to get Relysis through. Inside the chamber he quickly dropped to his knees and rolled the body over. Pulling the book the mayor clutched to him aside he put his ear to the fallen's chest.

"It's the mayor, his heart beats if only barely. Send for the healer," he called out into the hall to the guard beyond. The sound of boots on the stone disappearing into the distance the only reply he received to his order.

Checking for any obvious injury, finding none, he grabbed the mayor's jacket and pulled him away from the door. Once the path the healer would need to get into the room was clear and he determined there was nothing more he could do for Tralee, he began to look about for any clue to explain this second victim of what appeared to be a similar attack. His eyes immediately fixed on the book he had pulled from Tralee's hand and tossed aside.

He recognized it as Rathlin's spell book now that he had a moment to look at it closely. Walking slowly towards where the book lay on the floor he circled it once before reaching out his foot and nudging it carefully with his boot. Immediately leaning away from it as if he expected it to lash out at him, reflexively he held up a hand to protect himself.

Peeking around, and through, his thick fingers, he relaxed his tensed muscles when he saw the book still lying on the floor exactly how he left it.

Not ready to pick it up yet, he squatted down to look at it more closely as questions flooded his mind. Why was Tralee clutching it so tight, even as he lay in a deep slumber that appeared to be the same as Samuel's? There had to be a connection, though at that moment the healer and his staff arrived and chased all other thoughts from the general's mind. His attention was pulled back to the mayor as the healer began asking questions.

"Did you witness his collapse?"

"No, he was unconscious when I arrived this morning."

"Has he been moved?"

"Just from behind the door, he was slumped against it when I tried to enter."

"Anything else that you can tell me?"

Relysis paused for a moment debating whether to mention the book of spells the mayor was clutching when he found him, but decided to keep that to himself for now. "No, I checked to make sure his heart still beat and then sent for help."

Relysis kept out of the way while the healer examined the mayor as thoroughly as possible in the king's chamber, waiting until they had lifted the mayor onto a stretcher before he asked the question he could no longer keep at bay. "So is it the same as which afflicts the king?"

"There appears to be no sign of a struggle. His condition mirrors that of the king and his body similarly lacks any bruises. I will continue to search for a cause for their conditions when we get him to the hospital ward."

"I'll check on them later. If you learn anything before then, have me found." Relysis could see the healer was in a hurry to get the mayor back to the hospital ward so he didn't keep him any longer with more questions, but added a final request. "If he speaks, says anything while he slumbers, write it down."

Relysis was alone again as the mayor was whisked out of the room and down the hall by the healer and his staff. Closing the door behind them to keep any of the curious from wandering in, he paced back to stand over the book that still lay on the floor. Eventually he found a chair and pulled it over so he could continue his inspection without daring to touch it. He was still sitting there in deep contemplation when the door opened and Willos walked in.

"I heard about Mayor Tralee. By all reports he is in the same condition as the king, which I suppose is good considering the alternative." Willos paused as he looked at the general who hadn't yet looked up at him. "Can you hear me, are you in a trance too?" He reached out to touch the general, but stopped just short when Relysis broke the silence.

"There seems to be a secret within your pages that you have been so clever to conceal. The Mayor figured it out. I almost feel like he meant to, though the result wasn't what he expected." Relysis didn't take his eyes off the book as he spoke aloud, ostensibly for Willos, but clearly his comments were directed at the book.

"Are you sure?"

"Mayor Tralee was clutching the wizard's book when I found him. He was trying to escape the room when it overtook him."

"We've looked the book over and there was nothing written in there that any of us could decipher. We don't even know if Samuel looked at the book, and for sure he couldn't have read anything by accident that triggered a spell if that's what this is. We do not recognize the language of the script."

"If you have another theory let's hear it."

"I know the mayor is a good friend of yours and has been a faithful steward of Drogheda since its rediscovery, but could he have been jealous of Samuel sitting on the throne?

What if he somehow poisoned the king and when it didn't do the job he came back here to get more to finish the job and fell victim to its effects."

"Bah, you said yourself that you looked at that possibility and cleared him already. No, you're missing the truth that lays before your eyes." Relysis jumped from his chair and went over to where the book lay on the floor. "The truth behind both of these attacks is hidden within this book. You can keep chasing your theory with the mayor, but I intend to get to the bottom of this and bring them both back to the living."

Squatting down he snatched up the book, no longer fearful as his anger took over. Yanking the door open he left Willos sitting alone in the king's chamber and marched out of the office, down the hall away from the High Councilman and his absurd theory. Relysis meant to prove him wrong even if it meant he too fell into this mysterious slumber.

The Ghosts of Pendar

CHAPTER SEVEN

"Now that we have all been introduced it is time to get out into the fresh air. I have been living well, existing, in that warren the dwarves call home for longer than I even want to consider."

"Hold on, this isn't even possible." Samuel looked around at his traveling companions, seeing them for the first time for who they really were. Names from tales he heard from the day of his birth along with those of Rathlin the dragon. "Every one of you is dead!"

Reaching for the sword strapped across his back he was immediately struck from behind with a blow that dropped him to his hands and knees. The weight of someone landing on his back brought him to his stomach where he struggled to free himself.

"Stay down or I'll roast you like I did those dwarves back there in the tunnel, and you don't have the advantage of already being dead."

"Rathlin, take his sword and let him up."

Samuel resisted as much as he could when Rathlin took the sword from him. A knee in the small of his back kept him from altering the outcome and soon he was pushing himself back to his feet no worse for wear except for the notable theft of his sword. He dusted himself off as he regrouped, realizing now more than ever that Dungarvan was the unequivocal leader of this band and talking to the others would be worthless.

"According to Rathlin I'm alive, he kind of let that slip. Yet here I am talking to you, who are most assuredly a ghost, not to mention just having been mugged by another member of your ghost crew. Care to explain how this is happening to me?"

"It wasn't my intent to let you in on the secret." The glare he shot at Dungarvan's son standing behind Samuel had the young king thankful that at the moment his anger wasn't directed at him. "Though now that it has been revealed we no longer need to hide our true identities and Rathlin can drop the spell of confusion that he has maintained."

"Is the spell the reason everything is so hazy? This has gotten annoying."

"Unfortunately, it takes time to adjust, it will grow less so the longer you are here. That is a part of the realm within which we exist for now."

Samuel shook his head as if he hoped to alter the speed of adjustment, though there was no appreciable change. "You failed to answer my question. Where are we exactly then if you're dead and I'm not? How can we even be speaking to one another much less walking the halls of Drogheda together?"

"We currently exist on two sides of a sword. That razor edge slice of time between life and death. The three of us," Dungarvan nodded toward Kropett and Rathlin, "are on one side of that blade, while you are a hair's width away on the other side. I created a spell that would pull your spirit into the underworld, yet leave your body amongst the living, though in the deepest of sleeps."

"So if I am not dead, what about those dwarves we met? Wait, did Rathlin destroy their ghosts with his dragon fire?"

"Temporarily. They will be back to their ghostly selves before long. I really have no more appetite to continue this discussion, we must move on."

Samuel didn't even have a chance to protest before he felt a firm hand on his back, pushing him forward in the wake of Dungarvan. "How about water? Can I have some now that I know what is going on?"

"Get used to it, there is nothing here that will satisfy your thirst." Rathlin leaned over and spoke into Samuel's ear, guiding him towards the door.

Samuel took one more step, turning his head as if to respond to Rathlin's remark, then spun quickly and rammed his shoulder into the chest of his caretaker. The suddenness of Samuel's action caught Rathlin by surprise and knocked him off his feet to land heavily on his back. Samuel leapt after him, going to the ground with him.

Landing on Rathlin's chest he took the opportunity to connect several blows with his fists to the wizard's face before he could lift his hands to deflect the blows. It was the opportunity Samuel was hoping to create and he quickly scrambled for the sword Rathlin had let clatter to the floor to protect himself from Samuel's unexpected attack. Rolling off the wizard he kicked his feet free from Rathlin's desperate grasps and Samuel crawled away from his reach.

Finally clear from Rathlin he spun about to grab the scabbard and sprang to his feet. Backing away, he created distance between himself and Rathlin who was just getting his feet under him. Crouching, as Kurad had taught him, he gripped the handle of the sword and readied to pull it free from its sheath.

"Stop!" Dungarvan's voice boomed in the small chamber, freezing Samuel in place. "You do not want to suffer my wrath. Hand the sword over to my son or you will regret your decision forever, and when I say forever I mean it quite literally. There will be no journey to the halls of Dagda when I am done with you."

"You've got no right to tell me what to do within my own kingdom. I demand that you release me from this spell or I will use the magic infused in my sword to send you into whatever afterlife is waiting for you beyond where you exist now. I can guarantee it won't be the halls of Dagda that welcome you home either."

"Don't be so sure of yourself, both Rathlin and I possess magic of our own. Who do you think taught my brother the magic that he bequeathed to you?"

Samuel fought the doubt that began to creep into his mind. He had never faced a foe who had a legitimate claim to a magic that rivaled his own. The one time he squared off against Rathlin he had been bested, the memory of lying face down in the muddy streets of Glandore a grim reminder of who he was once again facing.

Movement to the side forced him to shuffle his feet and he realized Rathlin was moving to get behind him. "Get back, over there by your father."

"My father? I'm no spawn of a wizard. Samuel, don't you recognize me? I'm here to help you get home."

Samuel's head turned slowly, the voice familiar even through the haze that dulled his senses. His eyes settling on General Halfthor standing just a handful of steps from him with his battleaxe in his hands. "Relysis? How did you get here? Where did Rathlin go?"

"Who? It's just you and me against the wizard and his pet gnome. Come now, if we fight together he will be no match for us."

Samuel turned back to Dungarvan who stood across the chamber, his hands at the ready, his spell visibly forming on his lips. Even still with the general, the two of them could defeat the wizard. The magic in his own blade a match for anything that Dungarvan could conjure, the question concerning Rathlin's whereabouts returned to his mind as he turned back to Relysis.

"Did you see the other wizard when you came in? He was just here."

"I think you're confused, the air in this rabbit hole will muddle your thoughts before too long."

"That's got to be it," Samuel agreed, trying to shake the confusion from his mind. "The air in... this rabbit hole," he finished Relysis' statement in his head. The truth of what he said revealed more than what Samuel's eyes or ears told him. The general would never demean the city of Drogheda by calling it a rabbit warren.

"Come now boy, you won't need that sword now that I'm here with my battleaxe. Take your hand off the hilt before you accidentally cut either of us." Relysis' imposter continued to slowly close the gap between them.

Stealing a glance at the image of the dwarf to see where he was, Samuel shifted his stance once again to face Dungarvan. "You're no match for dwarven steel. My father told me that tale many times in my youth. His blade cut through your spells and dragon hide with ease."

"Your confidence in your general's axe is well earned. I care not for either of you, nor do I relish a battle against the two of you. However, if I must I will, I just need your sword. Put it on the floor before you and I will release you from the spell that keeps you here."

"Do it boy, let's give him the sword and get out of here and get back to the living."

Samuel hesitated for just a moment, taking the sword in both hands as he appeared ready to accede to Dungarvan's demand. He squatted to place the blade on the floor of the chamber. Stopping just short before he turned back to the dwarf standing near to him.

"You've gotten lazy in death Rathlin, not even Relysis would call his home a rabbit hole or his king a boy." Pulling the blade free from its scabbard he bounded to his feet. A pulse of energy reverberated through the chamber before the blue tendrils of magic raced along the length of the blade. The sweep of the blade arced through the space between Samuel and Rathlin as Samuel pressed the surprise attack to his advantage.

Before him Rathlin released the dwarf disguise as he threw himself backwards away from the razor sharp blade that nearly cut him in two. Samuel continued to press his attack with Rathlin stumbling defenselessly backwards attempting to get beyond his reach and colliding with the wall behind him. Raising his blade Samuel rushed forward looking to finish his opponent quickly.

With his blade poised to plunge into Rathlin's chest the air about him suddenly shimmered, freezing him in place unable to complete the act.

"What a difference a moment makes," Rathlin said as Samuel stood, fighting uselessly to move his limbs against the force that held him immobile as he looked into the now smiling face of Rathlin.

"Get the sword back in its sheath. We need to get out of this, how did you so eloquently put it? Rabbit hole, before it's swarming with ghosts."

The sword was ripped from Samuel's hands and returned to its scabbard with Rathlin securing it at his own back while Samuel could do naught but look on helplessly.

"Grab him." The words came from behind him and gave no warning of the blow that was coming. Dropped to his knees, his head swam as darkness threatened to overtake him. Firm hands grabbed him and forced him to get to his feet and roughly guide him out through the Western door.

CHAPTER EIGHT

"Your father seems at peace with his decision to abdicate the crown to Samuel," Jade stated as she handed Isabel a handful of small sticks.

"I think so too. I wasn't so sure until we arrived at Tyvig's cabin, but then it was like he finally unloaded the weight of the throne. He almost stood taller and his wounds seemed less," Isabel replied as she stood up from getting the campfire going. The fire served to chase away the cool mountain air from the small glade they had chosen to camp this night and gave the three light in the growing darkness.

"How do you think your brother will do? He's still young, and this was most unexpected," Willow asked as she began to lay out her bedroll near the growing fire.

"He grew up knowing someday he would wear the crown so I think he has the mindset and the training. However, you are correct that he felt that he had many years before he would actually take the throne and I'm sure, just like me, he never thought it would be anywhere but in Pendar." Isabel trailed off as she struggled to imagine her home left in ruins from the dragon Rathlin.

"You'll be welcome to stay in the forest with us as long as you like." Jade spoke across the fire. "When the time is right we'll help you get you back to Drogheda."

"That time is going to be sooner than you think." A gruff voice from out of the surrounding forest had all three of elven trained scouts scrambling for their blades. "I beg you to not raise a blade against me," the dwarf stated as he lifted his hands in surrender. "I am sorry to surprise you, though I don't recall a time where I was able to sneak up on a trio of scouts of your caliber." The smile hidden behind his beard belied the bit of pride he felt.

"Hodges! What are you doing out here in the wilds?" Isabel hurriedly rushed over to the Guardian of Drogheda and embraced the burly dwarf before pushing him back to arms length. "You are indeed growing skilled in your woodcraft. We would most certainly have been set upon if it were anyone with nefarious intentions." She frowned, begrudgingly congratulating him on his success at getting so close to their camp without their knowledge.

"There be no ill intent in my tracking you here, though the news I carry from Drogheda is not any that will lighten your spirit."

A wave of panic washed over Isabel as her mind immediately flew back to the terror of the dagar raining fire and destruction on the dwarven homeland, the image of it stalking across the Galway Bridge towards her as clear now as that fateful day. It's eyes boring into her very soul, intent only on delivering her to her death in an explosion of fire.

"Isabel, are you okay?" The voice came from across the campfire.

"Sorry, yes. I just, never mind," Isabel replied squeezing her eyes shut to try and will away the image before focusing again on the dwarf before her. "What news forces you to track us across mountains to this clearing? It must be important."

"I'm afraid it is, Princess Isabel." Hodges' use of her formal title got a raised eyebrow from the princess as she adjusted her stance. "The king has fallen ill."

"My brother, Samuel, what is wrong with him exactly?"

"The healers do not know how or why, but he has fallen into a deep slumber from which they are unable to wake him."

"How long has it been so, and how much longer will it last?" Isabel blurted out just a couple of the questions that swirled in her mind.

"He was stricken for nearly a seven-day before I was sent out to track you down, and then another twenty-three days that I have been on your trail."

"Did he hit his head? Hodges I need to know more, what else do you know?"

"Mayor Tralee found him lying on the floor of his chambers. There was no sign of a struggle and we have ruled out poisoning, that is why it was decided it was safe for you to return."

"We need to get back to Drogheda." Isabel spoke to the small party in the glen.

"I cannot return, we are a stone's throw from the forest and I have been away too long already. The city is still rebuilding from the dragon attack and my brother is likely wondering where I am," Jade stated, drawing a frown from Isabel which only deepened when Willow spoke.

"The scouts too were devastated by Rathlin's fire. It's the reason we were all returning to the forest. I think it should be us who are disappointed that you won't be able to finish the journey with us, your experience is going to be missed."

"Duty calls to all of you, it seems." Hodges' interjection, seemed to Isabel he was trying to reinforce their decisions to follow separate paths.

"Let's enjoy one last night around the campfire before our little band will be forced to part ways in the morning. Do you have any good tales to tell? The three of us have started repeating ours."

"I've been on the road with no one to talk to but myself for many days now, a new audience for my tales would be most welcome, and I'll throw in embellishments and exaggerations for not an extra coin."

"I don't make a habit of paying for stories, would you trade a warm meal for a handful?"

"Eating something I didn't have to hunt, clean, and cook seems more than a fair trade. Though I think I may want to eat first in case my stories aren't to your liking."

"Will these do?" Jade held up a string of hares they had collected that day.

The meal was enjoyed by all, as were Hodges' tales, and the group found themselves still up sitting around the fire much later into the night than was their habit. No one questioned whether it was the dwarf's stories, embellishments and all, or the knowledge that this was the trio's last night together, but it was some time after Hodges grew tired and retired to his bedroll before the rest followed suit.

Isabel took time to toss several more logs on the fire to ward off the chill and hoped they would burn for most of the night so no one would need to get up and add more before dawn. Getting to her feet it was with a fair amount of sadness that she looked about at her companions knowing that in the morning that would be parting ways.

Saying good night she climbed into her own bedroll with her mind still active. She had been so excited about returning to the elves in the forest that anything short of that was going to be disappointing, with the exception of returning to help her brother who lay in a mysterious sleep. Her immediate answer to return to the dwarven mountain home upon hearing the news still rang true, and she didn't waver no matter the sadness that crept into the corners of eyes and leaked out at the thought of saying good bye to Jade and Willow in the morning.

Hodges had distracted her with his tales, but she knew that in the morning they were going to be heading back to Drogheda. Wiping away her tears she forced herself to push her own disappointments aside and try to think of anything that would have caused Samuel to collapse and not reawaken. Though she lay and watched the stars for longer than she planned she was no closer to an answer when she at last fell asleep.

Coming awake to the familiar sounds of the others breaking camp, Isabel realized that she had overslept and was in danger of missing her friends' departure.

"It looks like someone was up late last night."

"You know me well, Jade. I'm sure you can guess what I was thinking about," Isabel replied as she sat up.

"The sooner you roll out of bed and eat some breakfast the sooner you will be on the trail back to your brother. You never know, he may have awoken by the time you get there."

"I'll bring you the good news myself."

"You are always welcome in the forest."

After sharing one last breakfast together the elves helped Isabel pack her gear before they set off for the Falkner Forest. Isabel watched them until they disappeared in the trees on the far side of the small clearing and then hoisted her pack and settled it into position. Hodges, following her lead, did the same so together they turned and headed back on the trail they had both walked to Drogheda. It wasn't the direction Isabel wanted to go even the day before, but she knew it was where she needed to now to help her brother, and that was all that mattered now.

The Ghosts of Pendar

CHAPTER NINE

Mayor Tralee stopped at the intersection, the sound of the falls enticing with the thirst that raged in his throat, but the hammers on stone promised something he needed even more. Contact with someone, anyone, who knew the whereabouts of the king. Rushing down the hall that would lead him into the depths of the mines, he was suddenly knocked off his feet as a wave of blue light swept through the mountain.

Shaking his head he sat up and looked around wondering if there would be another. Fearful of gaining his feet again he sat for several long moments and waited. From what Tralee could tell nothing else had changed except the hammers had gone quiet at the same moment the blue light pulsed and had not yet resumed.

Unsure if the phenomenon would occur again, he crawled over to where his torch had landed as a result of his tumble. With his torch in hand he held it above his head and looked as far as the light reached in either direction. There were no lingering effects of the blue light passing through that Tralee could tell so he tentatively climbed back to his feet, holding tight to the wall as he did.

Leaning with one hand planted on the stone wall he took a couple halting steps, fully expecting a repeat of the sweeping light. He continued on like that for quite a distance until the urgency of getting to those who had been hammering overrode his fear and he let his hand fall free from the wall.

Running as fast as he could towards where the sound of mining had been coming from he ran for what seemed like hours, until he was forced to come to a skidding stop before he tumbled over the edge of the steps. Still swaying, he stood at the top of a set of stairs that spiraled down into the depths of the mountain before him. Carefully looking down he could only see steps downward as far as his light reached. Pausing for just a moment to catch his ragged breath, wishing he had a canteen at his belt, he carefully stepped down on the first step.

Unsure if there was a bottom to this set of stairs the mayor descended several hundred dizzying feet before he stopped again. Holding his torch above his head he squinted to see the way before him, then turned to look back up the way he had come, neither direction hinted at an end of the steps.

The steps continued on for a short while when voices began to rise up from the depths below. Tralee stopped to silence his own boots and possibly hear what was being spoken, but no matter how he strained his ears he could not string together any intelligible sentences. Sure though that these must be the miners he sought he continued down the steps until a voice called out from the darkness below him demanding him to stop.

"Who dares tread the steps to the mines?"

"It is Mayor Tralee of Drogheda," he answered as bravely as he could, though his voice cracked as he peered into the haze unable to see who the other voice belonged to. The mayor didn't have to wait long before a pair of ghostly dwarves emerged from around the curving wall on the steps below him, their suddenness startling even though he knew they were coming.

"Mayor, you say?" They were clearly still on guard and didn't relax their postures even as they continued. "At least you're a dwarf, but we've not had a mayor in Drogheda for all our days. Drogheda has always been ruled by a king, a dwarf king."

The look the two exchanged on the last comment piqued Tralee's interest so he girded himself with all his bravery and pushed through his fear to the question he desperately needed the answer to. "Have you seen a human in the tunnels who calls himself the king of Drogheda?"

"What do you know of him and his companions?" Their hammers shifted in their hands as they readied themselves.

"I know nothing of his companions, but his name is Samuel." Tralee paused for a long moment before he continued, unsure the repercussions of what he intended to say next. "Samuel Ellingstone, the king of the reborn Drogheda."

"Grab him, he's an agent of the wizards!"

The next moments for Tralee were chaotic and terrifying for the mayor as he was tackled to the steps by the pair of ghostly dwarves. Unsure what was happening to him in the whirlwind of movements, when they stopped he was yanked back to his feet, hands bound before him, mouth gagged.

"He didn't speak a spell, did he?"

"No, let's get him down to the mine." They were the last words the two spoke to each other and the last Tralee saw of them as they hastily pulled a hood over his head to plunge him into complete darkness.

Time had no meaning as he was led down the never ending steps, one of the pair pulling the rope that bound his wrists, and the other nudging him in the back with what the mayor could only assume was his hammer. Ghosts or not, in this realm Tralee found himself in, their hands were strong, their steel cold and hard, so he put up no resistance.

At long last they stepped off the last step and continued their journey on smooth granite paths that wound their way deeper into the mountain home of the dwarves. Voices carried on the cool air reached Tralee's ears giving him some hope there would be an end to their eternal march, though he had no confidence he would be any better received than by his current escort. The sounds grew louder ahead of them and then suddenly ceased as they too came to a halt.

When the voice called out to them he could immediately tell they were in a much larger room. His assessment was quickly confirmed when the hood was yanked from over his head.

"Who do you have here?"

"Says he's the mayor of Drogheda, Tralee. I think he's in league with the new wizard."

"Does he now? So Mayor Tralee, do you deny that claim?"

Tralee tried to back away from the dwarf leaning in and questioning him from mere inches away, the ghostly guard with the hammer behind him didn't allow him the space. "I can explain, Master…" Tralee left the statement open as an invitation.

"My boys call me Bruff."

"Thank you, Master Bruff," Pausing for just a moment he wondered if it was a family name of a miner he knew. "I claim not to know any wizards, however, what I have to say might come as a shock to you."

"Out with it then, we don't have time to tarry."

"There is much I should tell you, you might want to be seated."

"Bring him over to the table so we can all sit while we listen to this dwarf's tale. He'll decide his own fate by telling us the truth or lying through his beard."

There was a scramble for chairs around the makeshift table as the prisoner was led across the room and, ultimately left standing. The chairs were filled with the ghostly inhabitants from the mine. Resigned to his position, he held out his hands to see if there would be at least some reprieve from his bindings. To his relief Bruff nodded to the guard and he was quickly rubbing at his wrists where the ropes had chafed. Tralee was given little opportunity to explore his curiosity about how a rope in this realm could cause him real discomfort when the leader demanded he begin his story.

"As I said there are some difficult things that you will need to hear in order for this to all make sense. I ask only that you listen to the entirety of what I must say before you pass judgment." Getting a nod in response from Bruff sitting at the head of the table, Tralee continued on. "One question to you before I start, does anyone have a canteen that I could wet my throat with?"

Not a hand reached for the canteens that hung at all of their belts while Tralee waited for even a bit of hospitality from his captors. However, the closer he looked into their eyes he realized that he may have stumbled upon an answer to his own question and simultaneously the best way to illustrate to them what they had become.

"Dwarves where I come from would be loathe to withhold water from a guest, even if they arrive under suspicious circumstances. Do any of you have not a drop to spare to a fellow dwarf in need?"

"I don't see how this fits into your story, but no, we don't. They are all empty." Taking his canteen from his belt Bruff took out the stopper and held it upside down. "Nothing but dust in here."

"You must be awful thirsty. I only arrived here a short time ago and my throat is as raw as my wrists."

"I knew you weren't from Drogheda. Let's haul him out of here and be done with him." Bruff began to stand and motioned to the guards to grab Tralee.

"Wait, I didn't mean to offend." Tralee held his hands up to forestall the actions of his guards. "How long has it been since you felt relief from your thirst?" Murmurs rose from around the table and the others standing about, a few even shaking their canteens before Tralee pushed on.

"I bet it's been years." Some nodded their heads. "I would dare even say hundreds, if not thousands."

The Ghosts of Pendar

CHAPTER TEN

The sun was muted as Samuel stumbled out into the small hidden glade outside the Western Door. Through halting steps he shook his head to try and chase away the black dots floating before his eyes. He had been knocked senseless too many times in his past and knew he would surrender consciousness imminently. Fighting to remain upright next to his escort he pushed down the nausea that had his insides flip flopping.

"Give him a minute. If he collapses we'll have to carry him."

The voice floated to Samuel's ears from somewhere close though he couldn't focus on from where exactly. Who said it, or even where they were, mattered not when he was finally able to stop moving forward and could focus all his attention on gathering his reserves to fight off the darkness threatening to overtake him.

Samuel didn't know how long he stood on unsteady legs before the world around him finally stopped spinning, but he was thankful when it finally did. Not intimating that his head was clearing, he maintained his hands on knees stance longer than needed. When he felt fully recovered he slowly lifted his head, giving the clearing a tentative scan to locate those he knew were with him, finally laying his eyes on Dungarvan.

"Thanks for giving me a moment to recover from you nearly knocking me unconscious," Samuel's words came out laced with sarcasm.

"It seems that you've recovered sufficiently, however, I wonder if maybe you didn't learn your lesson." Dungarvan stepped forward as if to threaten Samuel with another blow and gave only the slightest hint of a smile when the young king flinched before him. "Let us be gone from here, we have a long way to go."

The Ghosts of Pendar

Samuel caught the wizard's quick glance at the Western Door before he pivoted on his heel and led the small group out through the winding path away from the hidden door. Samuel also stole a look behind him before Rathlin's not so subtle hint that he needed to get moving. Dungarvan was clearly concerned that they were going to be trailed, though Samuel couldn't imagine who was going to come for them, and the group of miners didn't seem to be friendly towards Samuel so he didn't allow himself to hope for a rescue at their hands.

The dwarf ghosts from a thousand years ago may not come for him, however, he had felt the energy from the sword release when he had drawn it from its sheath. There was no way to know how far that pulse had traveled for sure, but it had completely unnerved Dungarvan and that alone meant that it could have reached others in the mountain. It was a thin life line to grasp for at best, but with nothing else to cling to that hope would have to be enough to keep him going.

Another rough jab from behind forced him from his contemplation and he quickened his step to keep up with Kropett as the gnome disappeared ahead of him into the rock maze that concealed the Western Door from prying eyes. With each assault on him Samuel added it to the list he had begun to compile in his mind, it helped him focus in the hazy world he trudged through and stoked the desire to get the sword back. Without it he was defenseless and alone, if he could get his hands on it there was at least a chance to change his fate and get back to the realm of the living.

He would have to wait as the day stretched out giving him time to study this world of the dead. The sun still plotted along the same course as it did for the living, though he couldn't tell if time moved at the same pace. Assuming it did, he wondered if they would stop for midday for a meal now that the sun was directly overhead, he even considered asking before realizing that his hunger was likely not to be assuaged any more than his thirst. After a moment of consideration he decided to ask anyway.

"How far must we walk today? My legs grow weary and my stomach rumbles. Do you have anything to take the edge off my appetite?"

"You'll get used to it, or at least learn to ignore the pains the longer you're here."

That it was the gnome who answered surprised Samuel. The little gnome had been admonished almost every time he tried to participate in the conversation up until now. The fact that he had taken this opportunity to speak up gave Samuel an avenue to try to find some answers.

"How long have you been here? I mean in this other worldly realm."

"I've lost all track of time. I was deposited here the day you were born and now you're the king of Pendar so it seems that it's been even longer than I thought."

"So you just went from one realm to the other? How did you know you had died?" Samuel's curiosity was suddenly awakened and took over the direction of the questions, forgetting completely about the grumbles in his belly.

"I thought for a moment that I had survived that battle between your father and Dungarvan even though it would have been a miracle. I mean dragon's fire isn't very survivable so I should have known. The fire rolled over me and then just as soon as it started the pain and heat were completely gone and I was completely alone on the bridge."

"That must have been terrifying."

"It was, when I figured out what had happened." Pausing for a moment he looked ahead and behind, appearing to measure the distance between them and the other two before he continued. "But then there was this moment of release and freedom from my former life and the decisions I had made. Unfortunately it was short lived, when your father buried his battleaxe into Dungarvan. We need to hurry now, there will be time to rest tonight."

Samuel cocked his head as he watched the gnome scurry away ahead of him, not sure what spooked him. He wasn't sure how much Kropett had meant to reveal about his relationship with the wizard, but he had provided much for Samuel to chew on as they walked through this hazy land of the dead.

Dungarvan finally brought the troop to a halt just as the sun began to disappear behind the mountains, turning off the road and going a short distance to a small clearing. It seemed to be a familiar stopping point for travelers complete with a ring of stones to build a fire at its center. Samuel quickly scanned the rest of the glade, turning back just in time to watch as Rathlin squatted momentarily next to the fire ring and recited a spell calling forth flames from the thin mountain air.

"You are still the dragon I see."

"That's not a concern of yours."

"I beg to differ. If you and your father just turn into dragons we could skip all this walking and fly to where we are going. Actually, where are we going?"

"Neither of those questions are any concern of yours," Dungarvan interjected before Rathlin could answer Samuel's questions. Instead he produced a vial from within his cloak and offered it to Samuel.

"You think I'm going to drink whatever you give me? I'm already in the land of the dead because of you. No thanks."

"It will help with your thirst and hunger."

Samuel paused, considering, the temptation strong to drink anything that could even temporarily quench his thirst. "Sorry, I don't trust you. It's likely to kill me for real."

"Don't be foolish. This is for your body that lays in a deep slumber back in the mountain. Without it you will perish and then you will no longer be just a guest in this realm. Now take it." Dungarvan didn't allow him to refuse it again and thrust the vial into Samuel's hand.

Holding the vial up to see its contents in the light of the fire he turned it around several times. He hadn't considered what his body was doing back in his office, his last memory before arriving here. Surely by now they had discovered his body, but there would be no way for him to eat or drink if he was really asleep as Dungarvan described.

"I guess I have no choice," Samuel said as he removed the stopper and tipped the vial up, drinking the entirety of the contents. Waiting for whatever effects he would feel, for good or bad, he didn't have to wait long. Immediately the fluid coated his dry throat, easing the desire to drink that had plagued him since his arrival. That would have been enough of a reason to drink it, but the contents immediately filled his stomach and satisfied his growing hunger.

"Thank you," he said before tossing the vial back to Dungarvan who snatched it out of the air and tucked it back into the folds of his cloak. Samuel barely had time to watch as he suddenly felt the weight of their travels wash over him, staggering before a pair of strong hands grabbed him from behind and lowered him down to the ground next to the fire. He remained awake for just a moment longer as Dungarvan squatted down to look at him, straining to hear what Dungarvan said as the world went black.

"Sleep well."

The Ghosts of Pendar

CHAPTER ELEVEN

"Do you need a hand with your pack?"

"I'm fine Hodges, I've trekked this path not that long ago," Isabel stated as she swung the pack off her back and let it fall to the ground. "Let's refill our canteens, there isn't another spring fed stream this high in the mountains for a few more days."

"You do know your route between Drogheda and the elves forest. I'm sure I wasted much valuable time trying to find you."

"I would think that even finding us out here would be near impossible."

"It's not like you were hiding your trail, and I did ask about your passing along the way."

"I guess we did enjoy the comfort of an inn or two along the route."

"Your father passed along to me what you told him about the way you intended to go."

"Of course you would have stopped there. I think you should stop explaining, I'm growing less impressed with your tracking abilities with every word you speak."

"Hey now, three elven trained scouts somewhere between Tyvig's cabin and the elven forest, and I caught you all flat footed sitting around a campfire."

"Say no more, we're even." Isabel held up a hand to keep the dwarf silent.

"Even?" A hint of smile peaked through Hodges' beard as he pushed her further.

"I hate to use the princess title to win this argument, but I will if I have to. You never know, I may be the queen." Isabel caught herself before she said anymore. The realization that the only way that would come to pass would be the loss of her brother had a sobering effect on their banter.

"We can eat as we walk. I have some waybread in my pack from Drogheda. I wasn't sure how long it would take to find you."

"He's probably already recovered. I will probably be heading back to the forest before another moon passes."

Hodges didn't say anything more to her, instead he handed her the piece of bread he had promised before filling his own canteens. Isabel accepted it with a whispered thanks, her mind tracing the steps that lay before them and calculating how long it would take to get there.

"Mayhap we should quicken our pace."

"I'll do my best to keep up with you on my short dwarven legs."

Hodges' self deprecating comment garnered a wry smile from Isabel who took advantage of the opportunity. "I'll stop every night and light a fire. I know you can find me then."

Isabel had to skip out of the way to dodge a shower of water as Hodges scooped up a handful of and tried to douse the playful princess. "At least keep my supper warm until I get there."

"I will if I have to, though I would prefer to travel together and have you help me keep my mind off the unknown that awaits us."

"Agreed."

The pair took off at an easy trot so they could keep up their conversation and still cover ground at a faster pace. Traveling along the trails and roads that wound up and over the mountains and through the forests, they continued their pace day after day. They camped at night when the sun began to set to eat a supper of small game hunted along the way, awakening at the first hint of dawn to start the new day. It was while packing their gear and preparing to strike out before the sun rose above the horizon when Isabel poised a question to her travel companion.

"How would you like to sleep in a proper bed tonight?"

"My bones feel old beyond my years. How do you propose we do that?"

"If we push our pace today," her statement elicited a groan from Hodges. "No, listen, let me finish. If we push our pace we can get to the Wexford Inn before they close the kitchen tonight and afterward we can have baths drawn to soak our weary bodies."

"No rabbit on a spit? What are you waiting for?" Hodges quickly pulled his pack onto his back and left Isabel watching him trotting away from their camp.

"I'll catch up!" she called after him as she took a moment to make sure they had left nothing behind and their fire was out before following his lead. True to her word it was within minutes that she had indeed closed the gap and caught up to Hodges, even surging ahead to his dismay. They covered the distance in this manner through the day and, just as Isabel had predicted, they were climbing the steps of the Wexford Inn when the sun was setting over the distant mountains.

"Back so soon? I didn't expect to see you again until you returned home," the innkeeper greeted Isabel as she stepped into the inn and led Hodges to the bar.

"It was unexpected, but I have return to Drogheda. Roger, this is my friend Hodges, he came looking for me."

"Well met Roger, though I believe I was treated to your hospitality many years ago on another mission. You were a young lad back then."

"I remember a band of dwarves staying here when my father was still running the inn. That was a long time ago and I haven't seen many dwarves since. It must be an important reason for you to chase her across mountains to find her."

"Routine princess stuff really." Her comment elicited a raised eyebrow from her partner though he didn't dispute her statement.

Isabel could tell he was searching for more details, but decided it served no purpose to let him know what was happening with her brother when she herself didn't. Her fear was that it would be spoken of with the next patron who may take advantage of the situation. The dwarves of Drogheda were in the middle of a re-birth and susceptible to outside influence, especially if it was known their king lay in an unnatural slumber.

"How about an ale for the both of you? You look trail worn." Roger said, brushing aside her apparent distraction as he set two mugs on the bar.

"That's what I was promised by the young lady, along with a good meal and a bath to wash away many weeks' worth of trail dust."

"Roger, can you please bring whatever is ready in the kitchen to our table?" Isabel said as she tossed a few coins on the bar before she ushered Hodges off to find a place to sit in the crowded dining room.

"You better hope it's not rabbit stew or we're going to have to rethink this bribery scheme of yours."

"Sorry, I panicked." Isabel nodded in the direction of the bar. "Perhaps I shouldn't have said anything."

"Is he untrustworthy?"

"No, it would be innocent enough I'm sure if he spoke of our passing and reason to be hurrying back to Drogheda. I've just seen enough destruction in my life to know what happens when the wrong person senses weakness and decides to do harm."

"Rathlin was killed and his army scattered."

"He wasn't the only one in Dulin that would like to take advantage of the growing wealth coming out of Drogheda now that the mines are open again."

"The wizard was the only one who had the spell to become the dragon, and that book is within the mountain. Without the dragon there is no force that can bring harm to those in Drogheda."

"I hope you're right." Isabel was saved from Hodges' optimism when Roger brought over their ale and plates piled high.

"Turkey, potatoes, gravy, and a bit of bread to soak it all up. I hope it's to your liking."

"It certainly looks like it will be just the thing to fill me up. I would travel many days to get a dinner as such, in fact I believe we did just that." Hodges excitedly surveyed the dinner before him.

"I'm glad to hear that, I'll be back with another round of ale for the both of you." The innkeeper disappeared into the crowd on his promised errand, returning with a pair for each.

The pair ate in silence, their hunger after a long day on the trail refusing to take second place to any more discussion. When they were finally done, Isabel having eaten and drank all she could, Hodges finishing his own and any that Isabel couldn't, they sipped at their remaining mugs of ale. The quiet lingered a little longer until Isabel, starting to feel the effects of the meal and drinks, decided it was time to turn in to her room.

"I'll check with Roger and see if he has our rooms ready for us."

"Make sure my bath is warm, my legs could use a good long soak."

"Promise me you won't fall asleep, I don't want to have to fish you out in the morning."

Hodges only nodded and lifted his mug in confirmation that he would be fine if left alone to his warm bath. Isabel smiled as she went off to find the innkeeper to check on their accommodations. He gave her the room keys before hustling off to see to his other guests. With the keys in her hand she got Hodges' attention, motioning him to follow her up the stairs to the rooms above. Handing him his key she bid him goodnight before they parted ways and went to their rooms, only calling after him as he fumbled with his key.

"Do I need to check on you later?"

"I'm fine, it takes a lot more than a couple mugs of ale to knock me from my feet. It's these little keys, they weren't made with dwarves in mind."

"I'll see you in the morning. Don't sleep late, we still have a long ways to go to get back to Drogheda. I'm worried for Samuel, I feel like I need to get to my brother's side as soon as I can."

Hodges nodded in agreement and waved her away as he finally got his door opened and slipped inside. Isabel smiled as he disappeared from view. She wasn't as sure about his ability to remain standing, waiting for his door to shut and latch before she stepped into her own and the bath that awaited her.

It was just after her door shut that the door to the room next to her own opened slightly, a figure hiding in the shadows peering into the hall to make sure the hallway was clear before he stepped out. In a rush he scurried down the steps with his cloak billowing behind him into the dining room below. Pausing to speak heatedly to the innkeeper for a few brief moments before he disappeared out into the dark night.

CHAPTER TWELVE

Kurad pulled up on the reins bringing his mount to a halt as he came into view of the ruined city of Pendar, sitting across the expansive field that had provided any enemy of Pendar a clear view of its formidable walls. Those walls had stood as a successful defense of the city for much of its storied history, with the recent exception of the battle against the dragon Rathlin. As it turned out the thick towering granite hadn't been enough and the rubble that littered the field bore testament to its defeat.

Clucking to his horse he urged it forward at a cautious pace. The dragon had devastated the city and left no building standing, but that didn't mean there was no one still within the once proud walls. Scavengers would come looking for anything left behind that would be of value, and with the haste in which the city evacuated it was hard to imagine that they wouldn't be successful. His hope though, was that a delegation from Drogheda would have returned to protect the valuables and take proper care of those who fell in the defense of the city.

Guiding his horse through the blocks of granite strewn about in Rathlin's rage he wound his way into the city plaza. A flock of ravens took noisy flight at his appearance, the first sign that indeed scavengers were within the city even if they were of a different feather than what he had expected. They were here for one reason only and the thought saddened him to know its truth. Proud warriors fallen to the dragon's army had been left to the carrion feeders.

That there were no men or dwarves here taking care of their lost brothers was puzzling to him, but it didn't mean there weren't others there so he kept his senses on high alert. Pausing for a moment before he moved on, he tied his bandana to cover his nose and mouth to ward off the now obvious stench of death that hung in the air.

Riding across the disheveled plaza, he picked a route to the castle that he hoped to have less debris and prove more passable than others. The sound of his horse's hooves striking the paved streets echoed through the empty city, bouncing off the tattered buildings and announcing his coming to any who foraged ahead of him. The idea that he could silently slip through the wasteland of broken buildings vanished from his mind, likely already having alerted those treasure hunters he thought he would discover.

Pushing forward he kept his eyes active for any sign of movement within the hollowed out buildings. Flickers and hints of shadows at the edge of his vision had him on edge inwardly even if his outward appearance showed no sign of the apprehension that continued to build. Realizing that whatever was here outnumbered him many times over, he urged his mount to pick up the pace.

Keeping his goal primary in his mind he coursed through the city, backtracking at a number of spots when the roadways were completely blocked. With the route he was on coming to another dead end and his mount growing skittish, he took a deep breath and steadied himself as he knew his horse was reading him as much as the shadows that swirled in the darkness. With his nerves calmed he dismounted and led the animal through the crumbling doorway and into the husk of what remained of the building.

Inside, he was immediately cut off from the brilliant sunshine that had served as a sort of protection and now walked amongst the shadows that continued to glide away from him. Still unable to catch a good look at them, and beginning to wonder if it was just his imagination playing tricks on him, he made for the far end of the building along the path that revealed itself in the half light of speckled sunshine that found its way in through the missing sections of the roof.

With the entrance behind them dark and their exit a glimmer on the far end of the ruined building Kurad had no problem getting his mount to move forward at an ever increasing pace until he was running beside the horse and struggling to keep up with it. Letting it pull him along, they covered the distance quickly, the illuminated doorway growing closer and closer with every passing moment until suddenly the way before them was blocked with a curtain of dark shadows. Kurad pulled hard on the reins, bringing his horse and himself both to a skidding halt on the debris covered stone floor.

Pausing for a moment to rub his eyes as if it would somehow clear away the shadow figures that blocked his way forward, his next actions belied his apparent confusion as the years of training took over and his reflexes overrode the paralysis that tried to root him to the ground. Launching himself onto the back of his horse he took his reins and spun it about, looking for an avenue of escape only to find the way behind blocked.

In a split second he made his decision as his horse danced a circle beneath him. Lining himself up with the exit he gave the command to charge forward, pulling his sword free though he knew not whether it would find purchase in the flesh of the shadows who faced him. Bent low over the horse's neck he kept his blade close as the gap between himself and the unnatural forces evaporated.

With every ground-eating stride from his stretched out mount the figures hidden in the mass of shadows became clearer and more defined, revealing the true nature of what it was that sought to block his escape. The front ranks comprised of gnomes of all shapes and sizes, behind them the massive trolls of Blackwater Deep. However, they were no longer the physical forms that had at one point laid siege to the city and broke through its walls, now they were the ghosts of Pendar.

A chorus of unearthly howls arose from the ghostly force arrayed before him as he neared their front lines. Gripping his mount tightly with his knees he gave it its head to find the way through as he held his sword at the ready and prepared for the collision with the shadows barring his way. He couldn't imagine what the impact was going to be like and was unprepared when he made contact with the broiling mass.

Shadow figures were blasted away as his horse barreled into their front lines with the ghosts sent swirling about as they fought to coalesce back to their forms to help in the attack. His sword sliced through the ghosts as they clutched at him, their hands ripping the sleeves from his jacket, drawing long rivulets of blood along his arms.

They were all around him as he swung his blade as quickly as he could to chase them back and keep from being pulled from his horse. The sword swept through their ghostly forms, dispersing them into a cloud of mist, but not sure if he was causing any damage that he could see in the frenetic battle. He didn't have time to look over long as a pair of trolls suddenly blocked his way.

Ducking down, he got as small as he could against the neck of his horse. Against this foe he knew he could do nothing but guide his horse past the ponderous sweeping hands that threatened to grasp him and pull him free. He held on as if his life depended on it, for if he was separated there could be no saving him. Just when he didn't think they would escape the pair burst out into the street and the sunlight that chased the shadows back into the buildings they haunted.

Letting his terrified mount gallop for several streets before he slowly brought it under control, he guided it to a stop and dismounted. Holding tight to the reins should it become spooked again he quickly rubbed down its legs to check for any wounds that would hamper their escape from the city before the sun set and no longer provided its powerful protection.

With his horse suffering no more than superficial wounds similar to his own he knew what he had to do. His original goal of checking on the castle to see what remained was gone. The only thing he could do now was reach the city walls before nightfall.

Leaping back into the saddle he began the arduous task of finding a pathway back through the city that kept them out of the shadows and clear of any buildings. With an eye on the position of the sun he pushed as fast as he could through the debris strewn streets of Pendar. On foot, he led his horse over piles of stone that earlier he would have found a different route to get around. With the sun growing closer to the horizon he finally reached the plaza within the main gate. He could only stop to gather his thoughts for a moment, sensing that the ghosts were congregating in the shadows, awaiting their release into the night.

There was nothing that he alone could do by staying in the city. The only thing he knew to do now was race back to Drogheda with this news. Samuel needed to know that a dark force had taken over the city of Pendar and would need to be dealt with, though Kurad couldn't imagine any earthly way to conquer this new enemy. Without looking back he put his heels to his mount and they raced out through the gate, leaving the ghosts to howl in protest at his escape.

The Ghosts of Pendar

CHAPTER THIRTEEN

Relysis was still muttering as he entered his quarters, slamming the door behind him to emphasize his current mood to anyone within earshot to hear the thick wooden door rattling on its hinges. Pulling the book of spells from his jacket he tossed it onto the nearby table before he yanked his arms free and threw it in the general direction of the coat hook on the back of the door where it landed in a pile on the floor.

"I know you are behind all of this and as Dagda is my witness I'm going to get to the bottom of it."

With the accusation leveled, he ignored the book as he stomped around the room for a bit longer as if to give the spell book a chance to confess. He set about lighting a small fire in the pot belly stove that stood in the corner of his room to chase away the chill ever present deep within the mountain.

"What are you concealing within your pages? Know that I will find whatever secrets you are hiding if I have to track that two bit wizard into the depths of the underworld."

The stove warmed up the room quickly and he began to cook a hearty breakfast of eggs, bacon, and toast on the cook top, never once even looking at his suspect though he continued to grumble to himself. With his plate ready and a cup of warm tea in hand he sat down at the opposite end of the table from the book and picked at his breakfast in silence. Appetite seemingly evaporated, much remained un-eaten when he pushed the plate away and focused his intense stare at the book.

"You and I are going to come to blows, I can warn you of that at the outset. Now, I don't know if your master can hear you but mark my words, I'm prepared to go to war over this unless you return my king right now."

Reaching across the table he planted his palm firmly on the leather tome and pulled it over so that it sat squarely in front of him stating for the last time before reaching his hand to open the book. "I warned you." However it was the book that struck the first blow.

With his hand still hovering over the cover it exploded open and the book suddenly flared with a brilliant blue light. Sending a piercing column of light towards the ceiling of his room, the glow bathed the room in its wonder. Startled, Relysis pushed away from the table, his chair toppling over backwards with him as he continued to roll to try and distance himself from the book's attack.

Visibly shaken, he crouched on his hands and knees to see if there was going to be another blast. Feeling all over his body for any injury, it struck him he hadn't been reduced to one more slumbering victim sprawled out on the floor. Unsure, but not convinced it hadn't been the same light that struck down Samuel and the Mayor, he replayed the event in his mind to try and figure out how he had survived its first strike if it was.

Everything about the event was clear from the moment he reached for the book and the light emanating from it except for the moment during the attack when it felt the mountain itself heaved beneath him. He gave himself a moment to consider the event before climbing back to his feet and righting his chair.

"Was that your best shot? Seems like your aim isn't so good when your victim is ready." Relysis cocked his head and tried to look at the book from all angles now that the cover was open and the text inside exposed. He was careful in his inspection not to read any of the words, instead looking for the burn marks on the book to be expected with such an outburst as he circled the table. His talk was tough, but he wasn't ready to try and touch the book again even though he knew he would have to in order to solve this mystery.

Sitting back down in his chair he steeled himself to approach the book one more time, foregoing the verbal taunting this time. He let his eyes skim over the exposed pages for long seconds before realizing the text of the book was in a language with which he wasn't familiar. Reaching his hand out tentatively to turn the page, he paused as he expected another flare up.

He shielded his eyes when he finally touched the page, cringing against the expected blast of light. Relysis relaxed slightly when the book lay unresponsive on the table. His courage growing, he flipped the page and once again brought the fight to the book of spells. "Do you have any other tricks to dissuade me now that I can avoid your attack?"

There was no response from the book as Relysis continued to flip the pages, every one of them written in a language that he suspected was elvish though he couldn't know for sure. Relaxing slightly the more confident he became that the book wasn't going to lash out again, he was startled when there was a loud bang on his door. Nearly jumping a foot off the ground the page in his hand flipped absently, falling open, the text swirling on the page as he stepped away.

"Who's there? Come in," he said as he walked to the door and opened it to reveal Willos' assistant Birr standing there.

"Are you okay?"

"I am, why do you ask?"

"The tremor, it shook the entire mountain, didn't you feel it?"

"I might have." Relysis looked over his shoulder at the book lying on the table.

"The council is meeting to enact mandatory checks on everyone. As General we need you to order the army to do searches."

"Let me grab my jacket, I'll walk with you." Stooping down he gathered it up from the pile that lay behind the door, pulling it on as he closed the door behind him, stealing one more look at the book before he did.

The pair walked along, Relysis more than willing to let Birr run through the lists of actions that needed to be completed in relation to the tremor. He himself had more of his own questions, at the forefront was one he hoped Birr could answer.

"Birr, were you in the room when they opened the wizard's book of spells to inspect its contents?"

"Yes, I was. It was rather unremarkable. Why do you ask?"

"No reason, I was just curious."

CHAPTER FOURTEEN

The horse's nostrils flared as it struggled to replace the spent air in its lungs. It's sides were heaving at the effort and its legs were wobbly beneath him. Kurad stood at its head stroking the frothy neck to calm its nerves while he looked down the road behind them, half expecting a hoard of ghosts to be on their trail.

They had galloped for as long as they could down the East Wall road to try and distance themselves from the ghostly inhabitants of Pendar. Kurad did not have to push his mount hard to get it to run, the howling that arose in the city that ushered them out was motivation enough. They had been forced to stop their flight when the sun set completely behind them on the western horizon and the scant light they had used to get this far was gone, the road ahead dark.

With nothing other than the stars above to light the way for them Kurad prodded his horse to begin walking with him. The horse was exhausted, but he needed to keep it moving to keep it from stiffening up. He needed his mount ready to go in an instant, the thought of the hoard charging down the road after them the only motivation needed to keep his horse limber. With gentle coaxing they were able to walk much further that night, going until Kurad arrived at the place he wanted to camp.

Even in the darkness he knew where he was, his elven sight helpful, his familiarity with the stretch of road proving just as valuable. Arriving at the old stone farmhouse hidden from the road as a result of being abandoned many years, if not lifetimes ago, he pushed a path through the forest undergrowth that grew right up to the walls and even within. Small animals hiding within the old house could be heard scurrying to distance themselves from the unexpected visitors as they made themselves at home.

After a quick survey to make sure they were alone he quickly had a small fire burning in what must have been the kitchen when the house still knew a family. With the fire lighting up the interior of the abandoned house Kurad removed his horse's saddle and poured a small amount of feed to replenish its energy while he rubbed down its tired muscles and checked its legs for any lameness.

After tending to his mount he found enough waybread and dried meat to make a meal for himself after he finally sat and fed the fire some more small sticks. He wasn't sure if the fire would draw any from whom he sought to conceal his whereabouts, the walls of the old house still contained most of the light within. Maybe it would keep the ghosts at bay if they did find him. There were no signs that they left the ruined city in pursuit, but he was not interested in them finding him regardless.

The fire had a hypnotizing effect on his tired body as he stared into its depths. He fought it for awhile as he continued to try and figure out what he had witnessed in Pendar. The thought that there may be ghosts roaming the world in an unseen realm was widely debated by scholars, patrons of taverns alike, though each had their own widely divergent theories. Kurad fell somewhere in between the two groups, willing to let the ghosts go about their business if they existed. However, a pack of angry ghosts physically attacking him had him shifting his thoughts on the subject.

His eyelids were growing heavy so he forced himself to suspend any more thoughts about the afterlife and did one last check on his mount. Removing the feed bag he made sure the horse was secure within the confines of the stone walled house. He also did another check of the perimeter to make sure there weren't any openings in the walls he had missed that would allow easy access other than the doorway which he had barricaded.

With his checks complete he threw a few more pieces of wood he had found lying about onto the fire, pulled his blanket over himself, and sat with his back against the wall in a creaky old chair. He wasn't under the illusion the meager amount of wood he had gathered was going to burn all night, but if it lasted until close to dawn that would be good enough. He intended to be up and on the road before the sun rose.

The fire had died down to embers when his eyes opened, his body tense though he didn't know yet what had triggered the response. There was barely a faint glow from what remained of the fire and it did nothing to penetrate the blanket of darkness that still lay over the old farmhouse. Holding still, he strained his ears to try and locate the source of alarm.

His horse shifted its feet nervously, confirming there was indeed something prowling the forest surrounding the old homestead. He just couldn't see or hear it yet and that was unsettling considering the ghost army he had witnessed in Pendar. An unnatural gust of wind carried with it the sounds of many souls nearby. Kurad used it to cover the sound of his blade sliding free of his scabbard as he threw back his blanket and sprang to his feet.

His reaction unleashed a cacophony of howls that ripped away the veil of silence that had lay over the property. Kicking at the embers produced a shower of sparks that spread towards the door, igniting piles of leaves that quickly dotted the small room. They flared quickly in small bursts revealing a surge of shadowy figures attempting to press forward through the door.

Howling at the barricade of fire, the ghostly apparitions shrank back from the light, out the doorway, and into the night. Kurad took his cue and added whatever materials he could find to the fire to buy him time. Smashing the old chair into pieces, he rushed forward and constructed a more formidable fire in front of the door, scooping up the burning leaves and heaping them onto his kindling. Dragging a broken table across the room, he shoved that into the fire too.

With the fire burning high in front of the door he took the scant time it bought him to saddle his horse and gather his gear in case the opportunity presented itself to get free of the stone house, though it didn't look promising. The howling grew louder again at the doorway and Kurad realized the fire had burned down faster than he anticipated, the wood from the old chair not lasting nearly as long as he needed.

Scanning the room he saw there was nothing left to burn and immediately ran to the bedroom where he remembered another small dresser still stood. There was a drawer missing, another broken, which was likely the reason it had been left behind. He didn't care the reason, but quickly drug it out into the outer room.

The table still burned in the doorway and when he broke up the dresser and added it to the blaze the desperate cries from outside grew louder. As much as they hated the fire, Kurad knew it was just a matter of time before it dwindled to nothing, and when the light from the fire died out his position would be overrun with by the pack of ghosts that had tracked him from Pendar. Time was running out and he didn't have any idea how he was going to fight his way free.

Unease crept into his mind. It was a new feeling for him and he didn't know what to do with it. Whispers from the bedroom caught his ear and pulled him back from the helplessness threatening to take hold. The ghost creatures had discovered the window hidden in the undergrowth, and though he couldn't tell the force of the attack, he had to assume it would be more than a mere feint.

Checking the fire he determined there wasn't much time remaining before it failed to hold back the ghosts. He also knew it was likely those outside the bedroom window were waiting for the fire to go out before they rushed in as well as those out front. It was clear they meant to trap him between the two and overwhelm his defenses. It was up to him to find a way past both, but when the last board from the dresser tilted and fell away from the fire his time to figure a way through ran out.

Gripping his sword, and guiding his distressed mount to stand behind him, the cries from both groups of ghosts rose to new levels as they realized their prey was nearly within their grasp. Shadows lunged at the door and fell back testing the effects of the fire, growing bolder with every attempt. First one, then another followed through the doorway, then the flood rushed forward.

With his blade held out before him he held a hand on his horse to keep it behind him. It suddenly screamed out in terror, its frightened cry piercing the air and drowning out even the howls of those that swarmed the building. Its terror so overpowering, it nearly crushed Kurad with its hooves as it bolted forward into the night and away from the stone farmhouse.

The Ghosts of Pendar

CHAPTER FIFTEEN

"I can't believe how much has been accomplished since I left." Isabel remarked to Hodges as they walked through the Valley Gate into the village. Her eyes were everywhere at once trying to take it all in.

"Remember, you have the entire city of Pendar working on cleaning up and rebuilding."

"When you put it that way it almost seems to be a necessity. Not everyone is comfortable living underground."

"Technically it is in the mountain, not underground."

"You're splitting hairs. Answer me this, can you see the sky when you look up, or feel the warmth on your face on a sunny day?"

"I cannot argue that point, however, I do think we need to forego any more discussions until we get into the city."

Isabel stopped and let the dwarf continue walking ahead of her so she could look around and enjoy one more moment in the sun, soaking up as much of the warmth. When she noticed him speaking with a guard, she hurried to catch up where Hodges waited for her at the Valley Gate.

"I have sent word to the High Council that you have arrived," Hodges said as he ushered her quickly past the guard post before she could ask them any questions, leaving the dwarves standing at attention until she was well beyond them.

"I wanted to ask the guards if they have any word of my brother's condition? What is the rush?"

"There has been a new development. The mayor has also fallen under the mysterious spell. Without knowing the cause you are to be taken immediately to the royal quarters to await a meeting with Willos."

Isabel didn't ask any more questions as Hodges led her through the tunnels, the citizens of Drogheda clearing a path for them as they hurried along. Exchanges between her and those they passed were minimal with Isabel getting only polite responses to her greetings. It didn't take long to pick up on their concern for the health of her brother, and in kind, her own apprehension grew the longer they walked. So it was with some relief when she arrived at her room and stepped inside.

"Mother! I had no idea you were here. I'm so glad to see you, is Father here too?"

"Hodges stopped by Tyvig's cabin on his way to find you. He must not have told you he saw us there."

"He did, but not that you were coming here." Isabel turned to the sturdy dwarf standing near the door, a somewhat failed attempt at a sheepish grin on his face.

"Your father is meeting with the High Council. He will be back soon. Have you gone to the hospital ward yet?"

"We came straight here. How are they doing?"

"They both twitch and mumble in their sleep and no one knows how to wake them." Jessica began to cry, burying her face in her hands. Isabel stepped close to give her mother a hug and waited for the tears to pass as she fought to hold her own at bay, giving her mother time to compose herself before she offered her some hope.

"I'm sure there is a reason for their slumber and we will figure it out. Who else has answered the call to come to Drogheda to help? Is Kurad here? He has traveled the far corners of Dulin and may have seen or heard of this affliction, perhaps he can offer some guidance."

"There has been no word from him since he left to go back to Glandore."

"That's been months, I would expect we will see him soon. He's always had a special bond with the kings of Pendar, both father and grandfather. There could be a chance that he now shares that with Samuel too."

"If that's true then he should be here already." The desperation in Jessica's voice made it sound like an accusation.

"Kurad has never failed our family, I don't think he will now."

"You're right about him."

"Father!" Isabel couldn't bend to decorum at the sight of her father coming through the door and rushed to him.

"It's good to see Hodges found you and brought you back to us, we're going to need your help."

"Do you have a plan?" She freed herself from his bear hug. "Let's hear it."

"We have a plan yet, but it's not widely known. Actually, he's only told me." Edward paused, looking to Hodges standing by the door, who feigned covering his ears before Edward continued. "General Relysis has a theory about the wizard's spell book being at the root of the unnatural sleep. It was at the scene when they found Samuel and Tralee was gripping it tight when Relysis discovered him."

"Where is it now?"

"Relysis has it in his quarters and he's been probing it for any clues, however the last time he read it there was a tremor within the mountain and a flash of blue light. He has it covered with a blanket so it can't see him. I don't know how a book would see him, those were his words."

"A bright light and the mountain shaking couldn't be any more obvious, clearly he has figured out something. Can we go there now and see if we can see what happens if we remove the blanket?"

"I can't imagine you would think that is a good idea. Maybe we shouldn't have brought you back here." The former queen looked thoughtful. "You should have stayed safe with the elves."

"Mother, they did bring me back so let's do something now that I'm here. And if you think training and living with the elves in the forest is safe." She regretted saying the last as soon as it passed her lips and quickly tried to push past it. "What else do they know about Samuel's quarters when they found him? Maybe there is something there for me to look at with a fresh set of eyes?"

"I can escort the princess to the king's chambers if that's okay."

"Thanks Hodges, I'll go get the general and meet you there."

Isabel didn't give her mom time to change her father's mind, immediately rushing out the door and dragging Hodges with her. "Thank you, I owe you. Now let's get as far from here as we can."

"What are friends for? You seemed to need some help."

"Now if you could read my mind and stop me from saying dumb things in front of my mother that would be even better."

"Sorry princess, I have my limitations."

"Don't worry about it, we're free now to go check out Samuel's quarters. There must be some clues there that will help us figure it out."

Samuel's chambers were nearby so the pair arrived without further discussion on what they hoped to find within and, after a brief exchange with the guard posted outside, they quickly stepped inside. Continuing their silence they stood side by side and tried to take in all the details, hoping to find something that had been missed by an untold number of others with the same hope.

With their initial survey over they began to walk around the room. Parting from one another, they circled in opposite directions, passing without exchanging a word until they both ended up together where they started.

"Do you see anything? Anything that is out of place, or suspicious?"

"Sorry Princess, I don't."

"I was hoping you had because I don't see anything that could tell us what happened in here."

"Maybe the clue is that there is nothing to see. If a fellow dwarf had been in here meaning to do harm, twice, there would be evidence of their coming and going."

"You're right, which means Relysis is correct that it is related to the book of spells. Where are those two?"

Though she was impatient to talk to the general Hodges convinced her to stay in Samuel's chambers until Edward and Relysis arrived, however, the questions barely waited until the door closed behind them.

"Have you been able to make any sense of this? It doesn't appear anything is out of the ordinary."

"Actually, I have. There are a few clues, one is the missing sword. Ah, you didn't notice its absence." Relysis chuckled at Isabel when her head spun about looking for it.

"No, you won't find it. No one knows where it's at and that is my first bit of evidence. The second is the book of spells found lying on the floor when Samuel's body was discovered, though that wasn't directly linked to the mysterious slumber. Mayor Tralee, however, was clutching the wizard's book when I found him."

"And you had your own experience with the book, but did not fall into the trap."

"I did, your father must have told you."

"You spoke of a tremor and a bright blue light."

"Both of those are true, however, neither happened when Willos and his assistant examined the book."

"Did anyone speak to the healer or his assistant as to what happened during the tremor? Did Samuel's condition change?"

"He struggles in his sleep from time to time, but during the tremor it was exaggerated. Where are you going with this?"

"Is the mayor's experience the same?"

"Not at all. Why do you think that is?"

"So they are having the different experiences, though they seem to be in the same place."

"Of course they are in the same place, they both lay in the hospital ward." Hodges interjected into the conversation between Isabel and the General.

"I don't think so, I mean yes, physically. Relysis, did the light from the book remind you of anything? Something missing that we can't find anywhere in Drogheda." Isabel moved to look directly into Relysis' eyes almost willing him to give her the answer she wanted.

"Samuel's sword!"

"It must be in the book and it reacted to something that happened, and if it is then so is Samuel, and Tralee."

"How do we get them out?" Edward asked the pair still locked eye to eye.

"I have no idea," Isabel said as she turned to face her father, "but I'm going to get him back."

CHAPTER SIXTEEN

"Where am I?" Samuel asked as he tried to lever himself up from the bed he found himself on, though he couldn't sit up completely due to the bindings that secured him. Frustrated, he flopped back on the bed and looked over helplessly at the little gnome who stood watch over him.

"How much time has passed? Never mind, it doesn't seem as if time matters here, but what did he really give me to drink?"

"Let's see, first questions first. We are at the Lost Souls Inn, and you've been asleep for a couple of days. Unfortunately, I don't know what that was that he gave you, though we can guess it was a liquid conjured from his book of spells."

"That name, Lost Souls Inn, it seems appropriate considering our circumstances, but isn't that a real inn?"

"It certainly is, though there is a parallel of the two different worlds. What happens in our existence doesn't bleed through to the living, at least not yet."

"So there it is. What is your master planning, Kropett?"

"He tells me little and trusts me to do nothing beyond his menial tasks."

"Why don't we team up and escape? We could go back to Drogheda and undo this spell."

"There is nothing in that book of spells that will save me. Dungarvan has the key to returning to the land of the living, so no matter what you offer me it will not compare to that opportunity."

Samuel broke off the conversation knowing there was nothing he could say in that moment that would get the little gnome to help him get away from his captors. Flopping back fully on the bed he listened to the sounds from the tavern drifting up through the floor. He wondered if the patrons below were like the ghosts whose company he was forced to endure.

"Why do people still congregate in taverns such as this? The ale doesn't quench your thirst, and the food tastes like nothing." Rathlin's lip curled in disgust as he tossed his knife back on the platter.

"Habits mostly. Some don't fully comprehend what happened to them so they keep doing the same they did in life. I guess it's comforting, though I would deem it just more wasted time."

"Then why are we here? This can't have anything to do with your plan."

"It very much does. We are waiting for an agent in my employ. I asked him to meet us here to tell me what he has learned from the living." Dungarvan looked about the room again hoping that his informant would somehow have materialized since his last scan of the patrons. A fight broke out among the patrons and the ensuing scuffle obscured his vision when the combatants squared up and the rest of those in the tavern joined in the melee.

The two wizards got out of the way as one of the ghosts crashed into their table sending their half eaten plates of food clattering to the floor. Dungarvan guided Rathlin off to the side of the room where they waited patiently for those engaged in the fight to bring the scuffle to an end. Eventually the ghosts who had joined in to support their man drifted off, having lost interest or realized nothing would be resolved.

Dungarvan took advantage of the shift in the crowd and procured a table closer to the door so he could more easily keep an eye on who came and went from the common room. The pair sat in quiet contemplation as the night continued its march towards dawn. The common room cleared out as the sun began to hint of its rising, the ghosts wandering off to pass yet another day in a never ending series of the same, pursuing that which they did when they still lived and breathed.

"Let's get going, your spy isn't coming today." Rathlin began to get to his feet.

"Patience, I can sense that he is close. It will be only a moment or two before he arrives." Dungarvan put a steadying hand on Rathlin's arm to reinforce his request. His son hesitated for just a moment before he settled into his chair. Then, on cue, the door opened and a man nearly hidden in shadows slunk inside and looked about furtively.

"That must be him."

"It is indeed." Dungarvan answered before beginning to recite a spell, the air surrounding the wizard shifting as he finished to reveal themselves to his informant.

"There you are, I was afraid I missed you," the man said as the wizards emerged from the haze and he approached the pair.

"Come sit down Tiberias, this is my son Rathlin."

"I had heard of your," the man paused awkwardly before restarting , "I wasn't aware you had joined your father."

"Good news spreads fast in the land of the dead, it seems."

"Oh no, I'm not dead. Your father must not have told you."

"It is true, Rathlin. He carries a talisman that I made especially for him. It allows him to see into the world of the deceased and interact with us for brief periods of time. To spend too much time here would trap him amongst us, so his visits are short by design. With that in mind, what news do you carry?"

Tiberias pulled out a necklace with a blue stone in the clutches of a dragon's claw and showed it to Rathlin before he began as if to prove Dungarvan's story. "I was watching for elven activity in the north as you instructed me when I came across the princess of Pendar, Isabel, on her way back to the dwarven warren. Earlier, when I was following her movements, she was traveling to the elven forest with a pair of scouts. I thought they had continued on and would be out of the way, but she was being escorted by a sturdy dwarf when I found her at an inn."

"So, what you're saying without saying it, and are hoping I won't notice, is that she is under the protection of a dwarf and there was nothing you could do to keep her from returning to Drogheda."

"You didn't hire me for my fighting skills." Tiberias unapologetically held up his callous free hands, speaking of a life spent avoiding manual labor.

"True, the girl alone would have been more than a match for you if you tried to confront her. The dwarf would have cut you in half with his battleaxe if you even attempted to harm her. I have another in my employ who is much better at those tasks. Hope you never hear his trademark whistle, it will mean your time amongst the living has run out."

Unable to dispute his master's assertion, and taking notice of the thinly veiled threat, Tiberias slumped back into the chair across from the wizard and seemed to accept his role until he suddenly he sat up and began to climb to his feet, eyes searching the room. "I need to get going."

"Relax, you're in my realm now. Nothing will hurt you here." Dungarvan stated and then with the man clearly distraught asked, "What is it?"

"I'm not sure, though I feel like I'm danger of being found out. Someone is coming."

Dungarvan paused for a moment and cocked his head trying to listen to something only he could hear. "Yes, you're correct, you need to get going. There is a force approaching that you're not prepared, or equipped, to handle. Quickly now, get back to the land of the living and as far from this inn as fast as you can."

Tiberias needed no extra motivation and quickly ran for the door, pausing only when Dungarvan gave him one last instruction.

"Meet us in Pendar, we will be there shortly. If you get there before us, tell my army we are on our way and have them prepared to begin the attack immediately. With the forces aligning against us we cannot delay." With the door still swinging closed behind them Dungarvan stood up and without a word to his son headed up the stairs leaving Rathlin bounding up after him.

"Grab your gear, we are leaving immediately."

Samuel jumped as Dungarvan threw open the door with a loud bang. Kropett didn't ask any questions of his master, but Samuel didn't have the same shared history and took advantage of the opportunity.

"You seem like you've seen a ghost. If that's going to cause you to bolt into the night, I have bad news for you."

"Rathlin, get your charge ready to travel by the time I walk back out that door."

Samuel cringed inwardly as Rathlin immediately jumped into action. The young wizard's favorite pastime was inflicting pain on him and he had just been given free rein to make Samuel comply. He was already tied to the bed and defenseless, but that hadn't stopped Rathlin in the past from unleashing his pent up rage.

"On your feet."

Samuel didn't reply, instead he held up his bound wrists and gave a half hearted tug on the restraints that kept him on the bed. In the next instant he was lunging backwards as a knife flashed in the muted candlelight, severing the cords that held him fast to the bed. Without giving Samuel a chance to get up off the bed Rathlin yanked the length of cord, causing Samuel to lurch forward and tumble off the bed onto the floor.

"I said on your feet. Quit resisting or this knife will sever something else."

"Gladly, could I get a hand up?"

Rathlin muttered under his breath while Dungarvan waited impatiently for the pair to fall in behind him. Stashing his knife within his cloak he reached down and clenched Samuel's hand, his grip feeling like a vice as Samuel gritted his teeth and accepted the help. Getting his legs under himself he clambered awkwardly to his feet.

It wasn't his intention, but in that moment the opportunity presented itself and, not knowing when it may again, he took his chance. The handle of his sword strapped to Rathlin's back was exposed and the temptation overruled any rational thought about what would happen if he failed. In truth, he had no idea what he would do if he did manage to draw it free, but he had to try.

Lowering his shoulder he drove hard into Rathlin's midsection causing the wizard to bend over with the blow. As predicted, this action gave Samuel a clear shot at the hilt and he desperately clawed at it with his bound hands, fighting to find a grip and pull it free. For long seconds the struggle seemed futile until at last he wrapped his hand around the handle and yanked it free from the scabbard.

Falling backwards with the sword in his hand, he watched as the magic burst forth sending a pulse of energy out across the lands. Maintaining his grip as he landed hard on his back, the blue tendrils streaking up and down the blade chased away the darkness in the room. In that moment the blade revealed that which had caused Dungarvan to panic. A force he feared threatened to disrupt all his plans was near now, the name coming unbidden to Samuel's lips.

"Kurad."

In that moment of enlightenment he caught movement out of the corner of his eye, though he detected it too late to avoid the impact of the fire poker Kropett wielded. It landed a direct hit on his still bound hands and forced him to drop the blade. With the magic ebbing away, Rathlin landed heavily on him and dealt a swift and brutal reprimand for his actions.

Samuel could do nothing to fight back and could only try to deflect the blows that rained down on him, the beating only ending when Dungarvan ordered it enough. Taking a moment during the assault he slipped off his ring and sent it skittering under the bed in hopes that Kurad would find it.

"The boy is right, we need to get out of here. I fear even now that we have delayed too long."

The Ghosts of Pendar

CHAPTER SEVENTEEN

The railing shook in his grip as he pulled himself up the steps onto the rough hewn boardwalk that seemed to dance beneath his feet. A blast of blue light made the night appear as day for just a blink in time in that very moment. The brief flash of light that accompanied the rumbling appeared to originate from the inn before him. However, it was gone in an instant, the railing growing still in his battered hand, the boards beneath his feet settling back to rest, and the light evaporating making him wonder if it wasn't just a trick being played on his tired mind.

Knowing that it wasn't just fatigue and his injuries causing hallucinations, but that something related to magic must have happened within, he moved forward faster than he would have thought possible moments ago. Pushing the door open into the common room he looked about at the sparse crowd, all of whom were looking equally startled at the burst of energy he had felt outside.

He was about to ask the barmaid what had happened inside when a faint voice called out his name from upstairs. It was no more than a whisper on the wind, but the look on the barmaid's face told him it wasn't just his imagination. He dropped his bag and took off as fast as he could up the stairs. There was clear desperation in that utterance from whomever needed his help.

Slowing as he approached the top of the steps, he silently drew his sword. There was a strong possibility magic had played a role in the light and tremor, and though his sword had no magically properties, it was elven crafted and would offer some protection.

Stopping just short of the landing at the top of the stairs, he stared down the dark hallway, sword at the ready, as he listened intently for any more calls for his aid. He was about to step forward, his foot just lifting from the last worn step, when the door nearest him swung open seemingly of its own volition, banging loudly in the quiet inn. Immediately bringing his sword up before him, he braced himself for the attack he could sense was coming.

The next moments added nothing except more confusion to his experience at the Lost Souls Inn. There was no attack and he saw no one in the room, but he had the very real feeling that he had indeed encountered a small force as they rushed past him. No, he amended, they had rushed through him, on their way down the steps. He turned quickly and caught only a swirl of shadows at the periphery of his vision for his effort. Whatever it was quickly disappeared even as he stared after the elusive images below in the common room.

With the door to the room still open, he knew he needed to continue on to see if anyone remained within. Easing over to the doorway he dared a quick look within before he swept through the opening with his sword leading the way. The room was dark and even his elven eyes struggled to see into the shadows.

Whomever the inhabitants had been, they left in a hurry and he hoped they had left behind something that could reveal their identities. Finding a lantern on the small table he quickly struck a light and held it above his head to chase away the darkness from the corners of the room. At first glance it seemed no one had stayed in the room, but he knew that wasn't true so he kept up his search.

Eventually, after checking the nightstand and bed, he began crawling about on the floor with the lantern held out before him as he felt the draw from a yet unseen object. Continuing his search for long moments, looking under every piece of furniture and behind the door, almost to the point of conceding there wasn't anything to find. It was then the glint of light off a polished metal caught his eye.

There was nothing within the Lost Souls Inn polished to shine bright under the scrutiny of light so he immediately crawled further back under the bed to scoop it up. With his hand clenched tight he backed his way out. Sitting cross legged on the floor, he slowly opened his hand to peer upon his find.

Even in the flickering lantern light he knew what he held in his hand. The polished ring crafted of dwarven steel with the familiar crest of the Ellingstone family shone back at him. This was Samuel's ring, and if it was Samuel's ring, then it must have been his voice calling out to him also, but where was the young king? The room was empty, and the occupants who rushed passed him seemingly were not of world of the living. His recent encounters with the ghosts of Pendar reinforced that belief.

Taking one more look around the room he determined there was nothing more to do there to solve the mystery so he pocketed the ring and stepped back out into the hall. Distracted before, he hadn't noticed the enticing smells from the kitchen and went back down to the common room below. Finding an open table, he dropped into the chair.

"Sir, you look like you have had a hard time of it recently. You must not have found anything up there," the serving girl spoke as she set a mug of ale in front of him and set his bag down next to his chair.

"You wouldn't believe me if I told you. Could you bring me a platter of whatever is ready in the kitchen? I can't remember the last time I ate." He emptied a handful of coins onto the table and the serving girl nodded, heading off to the kitchen. The chance to serve one last paying customer this late at night quickened her steps.

He did remember the last time he ate, though the events after seemed mostly a blur. From the moment his horse bolted from the old farmhouse and he grabbed the cinch strap as it raced out into the night his life had been a race to stay alive. Hanging on for dear life he had been dragged free from the mob of ghosts, but they had exacted a harsh punishment in those fleeting moments as horse and passenger rushed through them.

"Let me know if you would like another helping, and I'll get you another ale."

"I have enough to wash the dust from my throat. The room at the top of the steps is empty too, what do I owe you for a night's rest?"

"That will more than cover your meal and a soft bed for the night." She indicated the coins he had already proffered.

"Thanks, this should be enough to fill me up after a couple days of missed meals," Kurad said as he pushed the pile of coins across the table. Scooping them up, she slipped them in the coin bag at her waist and bid him a good evening.

Eating in silence before finally wiping the gravy from his plate with the last morsel of bread and tilting his mug up to let the last drop roll down into his mouth, he momentarily wished he hadn't refused a second mug of ale. Pushing away from the table he shouldered his bag and walked stiffly up the steps and back into the room where he found Samuel's ring. Dropping the bag, he eased himself down onto the bed.

He didn't bother to undress, his clothes likely stuck to the blood from his wounds and he didn't want to open them up while still on the road. There was also the possibility he might have to take flight again on short notice. It had been two nights since they had shown up on this trail, though he didn't know if they had given up the chase or were waiting for him to tire, and tired he was.

Closing his eyelids, he lay on the bed and was reminded of every bruise and cut he had received, both during the breakout from the old farmhouse, and the long punishing run by his horse with him dragging alongside, and at times, beneath with the hooves threatening to do what the ghosts failed to do.

The horse had been terrified beyond anything Kurad had trained him to encounter so he couldn't fault him, however, it had nearly killed him before he could dislodge himself and tumble free. As harrowing and dangerous as the escape had been it temporarily confused the ghosts and they were thrown off the trail for a day while Kurad had finally caught up to his mount and rode towards Pendar.

Both of them were bruised and beaten so they couldn't travel as fast as Kurad would have liked, but at least they were putting miles between him and the mob, or so he had thought. They came at them several times, though never got too close, his mount was on high alert to shadows on the prowl in the night and gave him ample warning to steal away into the darkness before they got within striking distance.

Then they had inexplicably stopped their pursuit two nights past, the relief coming just at the moment when Kurad didn't know if either of them could keep going. Since then he had pushed forward as well as they could manage, his wounds draining him of all his energy, leaving him numb to nearly everything around him. By the time the flickering lights of the Lost Souls Inn lured him in he didn't know if he could keep going. Now, as he drifted off, he wondered if he should have told the serving girl he would need the room for a longer stay.

The Ghosts of Pendar

CHAPTER EIGHTEEN

"If the history you just detailed is true then that would mean we have been down here a thousand years? Dwarves don't live that long, centuries for sure. Then what you say about us being dead would have to be true. However, if you're going to weave stories such as this to try and confuse us, we will toss you into the dungeon with the other wizards."

"All that I have told you is the truth and I do believe that we are all in this ghostly realm together. Wait, did you say wizards?" Tralee was caught off guard by Bruff's statement. There had been only a small number of wizards who had perished within the mountain.

"Are they friends of yours? It seems we have found the real reason for you sneaking around down here in the mines."

"No, not in the least. Do you have their names?"

"How can you say they aren't if you don't even know their names?"

"There has never been a wizard in my lifetime who was anything other than a threat to Drogheda."

"They go by Meath and Inish if that helps your recall, and I assume you will claim them to be dead also."

"It does, in fact. King Samuel killed them both, and his sword has been infused with the wizards' magic. They are the pair who nearly destroyed Drogheda by releasing the dagar." At the mention of the fire creature the entire assembly of miners gasped. With a start, Tralee realized that if others who had died still roamed the hallways the dagar could too. "Will you tell me if that monster is still haunting Drogheda?"

"We were aware of it for a time. The sounds reverberated within the mountain and we searched far and wide, but then it left suddenly and has never come back."

"That's because Princess Isabel, Samuel's sister, slew it with an arrow tipped with a shard of a magical stone." Tralee muttered almost to himself, reflecting upon the impact of the beast's demise. The magical shard had likely sent it back to whatever realm it came for and not trapping it within this ghostly existence.

"Another one of your royal humans?"

"Humans yes, but there is a rumor of dwarven blood in their veins, generations ago."

"Is that true, or just another of your tales?"

"It is no mere story told around campfires. There is a strength and grit about them that can only be attributed to a dwarven heritage." Tralee caught a hint of Bruff's demeanor changing and sought to capitalize on that nugget of information. "Samuel is tall like a human, most anyway, Isabel is not nearly so tall."

"If what you say is true then we have had a run in with him and his companions."

"Companions? Who would he know in this realm?"

Bruff's raised eyebrow reminded Tralee he had yet to succeed in his argument that they were all ghosts, but there was information about Samuel to be obtained and he didn't want to let the thread slip through his hands.

"He was with the wizard Dungarvan and his pet gnome. There was another with him we hadn't seen before, and we hope not to. He breaths fire as if he were a dragon."

"Rathlin, he is Dungarvan's son. He recently died in the battle at the Valley Gate. You must hear me, Samuel is in grave danger if he is in the company of these three. They mean him harm, though I don't know their intent in bringing him here. Samuel, and I too, are still in the realm of the living, but under the wizard's spell and laying in an enchanted sleep."

"You have given us much to think about, and the possibility has been discussed amongst us from time to time, though we have resisted believing we have died. If true, then unfortunately for us being trapped down in the mines means we are not dining in the halls of Dagda with our ancestors."

"How is it you came to be here?" Tralee was trying to be delicate.

"We were searching for the ore we needed to keep the smiths producing steel for our weapons and goods to trade. Some of us remember a thunderous avalanche before we woke up here. I guess we weren't as lucky as we thought, boys." Bruff looked around the room at his squad of miners, several with their heads dropping when the truth of their fate couldn't be ignored any longer. "Chins up boys, we're not done yet. The king of Drogheda, dwarf or not, needs our help and we won't be denied entrance to the halls of Dagda again." A chorus of cheers rang out in the small chamber.

The change in the mood of his ghostly companions caught Tralee off guard and for a moment he was speechless when they looked to him for guidance. Taking a moment to gather his thoughts, he asked, "Do you know which way they took King Samuel? Are they still within the mountain?"

"We're sure they escaped through the Western Door after we were attacked so I don't know where they are going." Tralee's shoulders slumped at the news, though with Bruff's next statement he recovered completely. "Let's ask the wizards we have, maybe they can track down the wizards we're looking for?"

"Yes!" Tralee wasn't even sure why he was so enthusiastic to see Meath and Inish, he just knew that he had gained some important allies who knew how to navigate this new terrain. He was quickly swept up in the stream of miners as they hurried from the room and down a narrow tunnel deeper into the mountain.

They marched for much longer than Tralee imagined they could, the shaft angling deeper and deeper to nearly the heart of the mountain. Just when he didn't think they would ever get there, the column of dwarves came to an abrupt halt. Calls for Tralee to come to the front had him inching past those blocking his path forward in the tight confines.

Finally emerging at the head of the column he stood next to Bruff in front of a dungeon door. The bars were constructed of dwarven steel as thick as the forearms of one of the sturdy dwarves who had crafted it. Through the slits in the door he could just make out the forms of the disheveled wizards sitting on the floor across from the doors. Bruff produced a key and slipped it into the lock, twisting it once as he released the mechanism. Giving the heavy door a slight push, he watched it glide open silently.

"Don't worry, they can't harm you," Bruff assured Tralee and one of the wizards held up wrists shackled to a thick chain anchored into the far wall. "We have a guest with some questions for you."

"I recognize this one. You don't seem like you belong here, do you?" Inish asked as he stood up, clearly struggling against the weight of the chains that bound him. "Come now, I can't harm you, the steel holds us fast."

Tralee couldn't help but hesitate, he remembered the power the wizard had wielded in life. Trusting Bruff, he took a deep breath before he stepped into the small chamber and demanded the prisoner answer his questions.

"Are you aware Dungarvan and his son haunt these halls?"

"Bound as we are, there are things that we feel, though we don't understand entirely." Inish held up his shackled wrists as if to emphasize his plight.

"You're never going to be released so you might as well tell us what you know. We have seen them, and even confronted them so we know it is true." Bruff couldn't hold back, his disdain for the captives on display.

"What if we released you? On the promise you don't linger in this realm." Tralee offered, quickly adding, "Or attempt to alter the world of the living."

"They are wizards and unable to keep their word."

"Inish may not, but I will. I'm tired of being chained in this hole endlessly," Meath said as he got to his feet and moved towards Tralee, holding out his wrists to have his chains removed.

"Tell us what you know and we'll consider it." Tralee's offer drew a sharp inhale from Bruff, though the miner didn't say otherwise.

"Those tremors you've been feeling are my magic. The boy, Samuel, his sword has been brought into the world of those who are dead and can't, or choose not, to escape this realm to what lies beyond."

"Do I have to remind you that he is your brother? He may need our help." Inish tried to dissuade Meath to no avail.

"He'll not get my help in whatever scheme he is attempting this time. My years here have been used up and if I can offer some help to stop him as atonement, it's a trade I'm willing to make. You should consider it too." Meath gave Inish an opening to change his mind.

"What do they intend to do with the king and his sword?"

"King now? There has been a change in the one who sits on the throne. Did some ill befall his father?"

"No, Edward abdicated his throne to Samuel so he could convalesce. Now, I need you tell us where they are going with Samuel and his sword."

"Fair enough. Though Edward was a worthy adversary I would wish him no ill will now that I've passed. The magic in the sword is powerful, you have felt the tremors, and I'm sure that wasn't even from the event that he surely has planned."

"So do you know where he is going? Can you feel where the magic is going?"

"I don't know where it's going, but it has left the mountain and is traveling away from here. However, if you can convince Inish to help us he can use his scrying bowl and we can locate their whereabouts."

"If you don't help us I will destroy the key to the locks that bind you in this cell and these walls will be the only thing you ever see for the rest of your existence with no one to share your misery forever." Bruff's threat clearly struck Inish hard, his face clearly showing the internal struggle as he was forced to contemplate the alternatives.

"Even if I wanted to help I couldn't use the bowl without water." Inish pulled his treasured magical item out from within his robes and wiped the dust from the bowl and tipped it upside down.

"Release me and I will fill it with water as my last and final act," Meath said as he held up his wrists to have the shackles removed.

Tralee motioned to Bruff to do as he was bid and within moments Meath was standing before them free from the steel that had blocked his magic for the last several years.

"Hold your bowl up." Inish did as Meath asked and to everyone's amazement the bowl was full of crystal clear water. "The water won't last long once I'm gone. Now do the right thing." With a deep sigh, he breathed in deeply one last time before vanishing.

"It's a limited time offer. What do you say?"

"I promise that if you release me I will tell you what the waters show me. Then I will follow Meath in search of eternal peace."

Bruff didn't need any instruction this time, instead he released the locks that bound the wizard and stepped back as the shackles fell free to clatter on the stone floor. There were long moments of silence as Tralee and Bruff looked on apprehensively, not knowing if the wizard would follow through on his promise.

"Remember your promise." Bruff broke the silence, shifting his hand so it hovered over the hammer that hung at his belt.

"That won't be necessary, will it?" Tralee held a hand up to forestall Bruff from reacting, the information that Inish could provide more important than anything else in that moment.

"Dungarvan travels with his son Rathlin, his pet gnome, and the boy king." The wizard paused for a moment as he appeared to struggle with helping those who would try to rescue the one that killed him. "It's Pendar, that's where they are going. The city is held in a darkness I can't see through, but that is where you will find them."

As soon as the wizard finished his viewing the magical water vanished into thin air just as quickly as it had appeared. With nothing more than a nod Inish too vanished from the chamber, his scrying bowl clattering to the floor, apparently unable to travel with him into the afterlife.

Tralee moved as if to retrieve it from where it lay before Bruff stopped him. Guiding him from the cell, he locked the door behind them and tossing the key within. "Best to leave some things where they can't hurt anyone. Now let's go rescue this king of ours."

The Ghosts of Pendar

CHAPTER NINETEEN

Kurad surveyed the Valley Gate village from the back of his horse. They had traveled from the border town to Drogheda as fast as he could safely push his mount, alternately riding and walking as they swung north and came in through the Curragh mountains. His goal had been to make better time above ground and not need to go underground as he would if he came to Drogheda through the Western door. In the end he didn't know if his plan had worked, though at last he was here.

He was still sore, but the aches and pains had subsided considerably since he had swung his legs out from the bed he found at the Lost Souls Inn. It was the last one he slept in on his journey, the hard ground every night since not as forgiving to his injuries. As much as he wanted to spend more time there, and possibly recover faster, he knew there was a mystery surrounding Samuel and that was more important in this moment.

Clucking to his horse, they moved off from his vantage point and made their way down the valley to the village. He was sure he was identified some way off when a dispatch from the gate was sent running back through the village, presumably to announce his arrival. As the throne's unofficial protector, a role he had assumed when Edward's father, Samuel had asked him to take the boy into hiding so many years ago. He wasn't going to slip into town without notice, but the speed at which he raced away caused him some concern and he called for his horse to quicken its pace.

"What news can you tell me of the whereabouts of the king?" Kurad asked of the remaining men standing watch at the wall as he pulled up on his horse, his hand unconsciously felt for the king's ring in his pocket.

"He's in the mountain." The guard's response both surprising and relieving to Kurad until the guard finished his sentence, "he lies in the same deep unnatural sleep as he has for more days than I can remember."

Kurad flicked the reins on his mount and urged it forward as quickly as they could go through the busy village streets. Calling out ahead of the pair to clear the way, he pushed for more speed, the need to get to the king's side overriding his concern for his mount's lingering injuries. The villagers scattered ahead of him as he pushed through to the Village Gate, dropping to the ground and running the last several yards. Not speaking more than a word of thanks to the dwarves standing watch, he tossed them the reins before darting in through the gate.

News of his coming barely beat him to the mountain, there were already emissaries en route to intercept him. Making contact with him they quickly guided him to the hospital ward, bringing him into the room where Samuel lay.

"I knew you were coming." A quiet voice came from the corner of the room Kurad hadn't noticed in his singular focus.

"Isabel." Recognizing the voice he turned to greet her, the young princess grabbing onto him in a fierce hug.

"He called out to you several nights ago, I knew you would be here soon."

"I heard him, and he left me this clue." Kurad pulled away enough to retrieve the king's ring from his pocket and hand it to Isabel.

"Where did you get this?" Her head spun immediately to look at Samuel's still form, his hands resting across his chest. "It's gone from his hand, though I remember seeing it when I first came back and visited him here."

"I found it at the Lost Souls Inn the very night he called out my name from a room above."

"That's impossible."

"There is other news I carry with me that would seem unbelievable in its own right, however, coupled with my experience in the border town and in Pendar I would have to say they are linked."

"You were in Pendar?"

"I felt the need to stop on my way home from Glandore and see it after the dust had settled."

"Is it as bad as I've been told?"

"Worse, there are new inhabitants."

"Someone has moved into the city?" A voice asked from the doorway, causing Kurad and Isabel to pivot toward it.

"Edward, I didn't know you were back in the mountain. I did not think you would be traveling. How is your injury?"

"The word went out about Samuel. I assume that's why you've arrived here too." Edward waved away Kurad's concern for his injury at the hands of Rathlin, one that had left him less than he had once been.

"Father, Samuel called out to him."

"Just now?"

"No, Kurad you tell it."

"Isabel is right. I was at the Lost Souls Inn, having just arrived from a harrowing ride from Pendar. As I stepped through the door his voice called out to me from above. When I got to the top of the steps a shadow passed me by, the energy was unmistakable, and within the room I found Samuel's ring."

Edward took the ring from Kurad's outstretched hand, turning it over to confirm its authenticity, his eyes straying to Samuel's hands just as Isabel did before he handed it back. "You spoke of a dangerous ride from Pendar, described in terms that I don't recall you speaking in all my years."

"Ghostly figures followed and attacked my horse and I from the time we left Pendar until shortly before we arrived at the inn."

"That's impossible, they hold no sway over the living."

"Something has changed and I feel like Samuel has been pulled into whatever is happening."

"We need to talk to Relysis, he has looked at Dungarvan's book of spells."

"Dungarvan is involved?" Kurad asked.

"Possibly, the spell book we found in Rathlin's pack was near Samuel, and Tralee was clutching it when the general found him in the same deep sleep that has taken Samuel."

"It can't be a coincidence. Where is the general now?" Kurad was ready to get to the bottom of it immediately.

"Likely in his office, I'll meet you there. I want to get my gear from my quarters." Isabel's comment earned a curious look from both her father and Kurad. "Samuel brought his sword with him, I'm not going without my bow."

The three of them were quick to leave the hospital ward, parting ways only for Isabel to grab her gear and then met back up to track down the whereabouts of Relysis. Knocking on the door to his quarters, they interrupted his continued inspection of the very book they were looking to discuss with him.

"I figured you would be showing up soon with Samuel calling out to you, in fact I've been waiting."

"You're not surprised then that I have this?" Kurad tossed the general Samuel's ring.

"Not in the least. It proves my theory that there is some wizardry going on here, and clearly Samuel needs our help."

"How do we reach him?" Edward asked.

"We read the book, which is why I've been waiting for Kurad to show up. Did your father teach you to read elvish? The book is written in an ancient form."

"I've gotten better, however, if it's an old version I don't know that I will be of much help."

"I can help." The other three looked at Isabel questioningly. "Jade has been teaching me. Training to be an elven scout goes beyond tracking orcs, and any others who cross into the forest."

"We were there on official business, and it was years ago." Relysis' defensiveness garnered a grin from Isabel.

"Let's take a look at this book," Isabel said as she lead the way to the table where the wizard's book of spells rested.

"Careful princess, one time when I opened it there was a pulse of blue light that shook the whole mountain."

"The same happened at the inn right before I heard him call out my name."

"What are we waiting for then?" Relysis suddenly voiced less caution than he had moments ago given the mounting evidence they were on the right track.

"Yes, caution young lady." Edward's fatherly advice tamped down the general's impatience.

"Wait." Kurad's voice froze Isabel in place as she was about to touch the book. "I don't think we can allow Edward to be in the room for this."

"Do I have to remind you that it's my son we're trying to find?"

"Only if I have to point out that you're the only living member of the royal family left if something were to happen to Isabel."

"That's exactly why I need to be here."

"Father, we don't know if anything will happen, but even if it does I'll be fine. I've faced greater threats than a handful of ghosts." Luckily for Isabel her father didn't see Kurad's eyebrows raise at her proclamation.

"I'll be out in the hallway, if I hear anything I will be back in a moment's time."

The three designated participants waited for Edward to leave the room before once again approaching the book that sat in the middle of the table.

"Are you sure you want to do this? The ghosts I encountered nearly tore my horse and I to pieces."

Isabel paused for just a moment, though it wasn't out of her own concern. Samuel had been gone from them for weeks now and by all accounts living in the realm that she was volunteering to enter in order to save him. She wouldn't want to be anywhere else in this moment. Without another word she flipped the cover open and began to scan the pages as she flipped them.

"Anything look familiar? Any spell that would turn us into those ghosts Kurad ran into?"

"Do you remember where you left off?" Isabel was hesitant to admit that most of the text was unreadable to her.

"Let me see." Relysis moved the book over so he could see it too and flipped the pages, perusing them as if to see if he recalled where he had been interrupted. After several moments he stopped turning the pages. "Here, it must have been about this far in."

"No tremors or lights yet, you're sure?" Isabel asked as she took the book back, turning one more page as she questioned Relysis. The text swirled on the page as they looked down at the book of spells, the letters finally settling in place so that they could all read them. Their focus on the book of spells, the mist gathered about them silently waiting to take them beyond as Isabel read the spell aloud.

Mist of the Mountain

The path lay before the stricken, the weight of the mountain pressing down on he who walked alone on his final journey with his sword at his back. The air swirled about his legs as he passed through the world around him. The haze before his eyes served as a distraction to conceal the truth of his purpose.

Edward waited outside as long as he could force himself to, the dwarf's quarters were quiet, too quiet for his liking. Finally gripping the handle and pushing the door open he took in the scene he had feared the most. All three who had been studying the book of spells were slumped to the floor as a whiff of mist dissipated before him.

Rushing over to his daughter first he quickly checked to make sure she was still breathing, and once satisfied, he moved on to the other two who lay nearby. Standing up, he turned to retrieve the healer so that they could bring these three to the hospital ward. It was in that moment the figure stepped through the door, shutting it behind him he let out a low whistle.

"I can't let you leave this room." He stated as his blade slid free from the sheath at his belt, the honed blade reflecting the light from the candle that still burned on the table.

Edward reached for his own belt, his heart sinking as he realized he had left it behind. He only had a moment to regret not following Isabel's lead in grabbing her weapons before the shadowy figure was on top of him. Wincing in pain as he tried to move out of the way, his old wound aggravated by his recent travels, hampering his ability.

Throwing up an arm to defend himself he felt the blade cut deep into his flesh. Bringing his other arm across he attempted to land a blow to his attacker's body and try to gain some separation. His fist never landed as the elusive figure ducked his ponderous swing, but he did achieve his goal of getting some distance between them. It was short lived, the next attack against him more fierce and targeted his midsection.

The assassin's blade drove deep into him, tearing open his old wound completely. The pain exploded through Edward's body. With his strength ebbing away with every moment as his lifeblood flowed from his abdomen, he tried in vain to push the attacker off of him. It was in that moment with the darkness encroaching on his vision, his arms growing heavy and legs shaking, the truth struck him. Tonight he would be in the same world as the rest. A grim smile creased his lips at the thought of that reunion as the world about him went dark.

With the blood flowing freely over his arm he held the former king of Pendar until he knew his mission had been accomplished. Letting the man slide to the floor he turned his attention to the others lying in their unnatural slumber in the room.

He had been told to take care of the king's protector if at all possible, so he approached him first. Voices growing louder from the hall stopped his action. Listening carefully, he knew he didn't have the time he needed. Stopping briefly to tuck the dragon claw amulet into his tunic, he blew out the candle and slipped back out the door to escape the mountain before any alarms were sounded.

CHAPTER TWENTY

"That can't happen again. If that boy draws too much attention to us we will never make it back to the land of the living. Do you not understand?" Dungarvan berated Rathlin as they stood in the middle of the dirt packed street outside the Lost Souls Inn looking back at the doorway they had just escaped out through. Kropett wisely watched over their groggy captive on the steps as far from the angry wizard as he could.

"I'm very sorry, Father. He took me by surprise."

"The fact that Kurad was here tonight is cause for great concern, and I fear it was not a coincidence. We must hurry now, the boy's protector surely heard him call out his name."

"I didn't think the living could hear his cry for help."

"The boy exists in both places, at least for the moment. It allows him certain abilities, if you will. That will change shortly when he has fulfilled his purpose, but first we need to get to Pendar and secure the book from the forces that still hold the city against my army."

"We have an army?" Rathlin's phrasing drew a quick correction from Dungarvan.

"I, have assembled a force of gnomes and trolls. They are the ghosts of those who died when Orgle took the city from the boy's grandfather."

"Who is it that they battle, what army could stand against your army of dead?"

"King Samuel Ellingstone, the boy's grandfather. He still protects the city with an army of dwarves and men. It is a battle that has raged since my death at the hands of his son." Dungarvan could see that Rathlin was confused, and if his plan was to succeed he needed his protégé to understand what had transpired since his own death.

"I'll tell you the story as we walk. We have much ground to cover." Dungarvan motioned to his pet gnome to follow them at a distance to keep Samuel's ears from hearing that what he meant only for Rathlin to know. With the boy king far enough away, he began his telling of the events following his death.

"After I was slain I made the journey to Pendar. I knew that I needed to get my hands on the magical tome they unwittingly keep in the library there so that I could search its text to find the answer to my release from death and return to the living.

Upon arriving there I entered the city at night, not wanting to risk running into any of the living who might have the ability to sense my presence. The city of the living was thriving under Edward. The king and queen had returned and a new heir introduced to great celebration. The dead took no part in those festivities, they were completely unaware, and in truth, would soon be consumed with other concerns. Me.

I thought I had slipped through undetected by both the living and the dead, but as I arrived at the castle and entered the library he was there to stop me. He knew the value of the book, or had deduced it.

'So you are why I am stuck here and not in the halls of the fallen who have gone before me,' he said.

'Give me the tome and I will release you to whatever awaits you after this.'

'You alone have no power to promise that, even if I would accept your invitation.' Samuel spoke as he grabbed his sword and held it before him. 'I'm ready to move on, though first I need to make sure you are no longer a threat to the living.'

I knew I was not ready to match him without my magic so I fled before him and, with the help of his fallen, they threw me from the city. I ran all night long as the dwarves chased me through the realm of the ghosts. They knew I was the reason they were tethered to the realm of the ghosts.

Before I got free of the city I came across pockets of gnomes and a handful of trolls who were similarly bound, locked into this struggle that had been foreordained. At first they didn't trust me, but soon I recruited from those who had died at the hands of the dwarves an army of my own. With my promise to release them they were all too willing to help finish the task."

"They have been awaiting my return ever since to participate in the battle for Pendar." Dungarvan stated as he finished his retelling.

"The city has been destroyed. I did it myself, there is nothing left of it."

"They care not about the city. Their fight is against the ghost king who still holds the castle even in the afterlife, and the destruction of his family line they were seeking to end while they yet lived. I promised them the life of the new king if they would help me achieve my goal of returning to the living. In order to do that I need to know how you are doing on recovering your full ability to become the dragon, not just the fire, the ability to take flight too."

"I grow stronger the longer I am in this new realm, though the air is so very different."

"Practice the spell, let Kropett watch the boy."

Dungarvan retreated to his own thoughts, concern that he would not have both dragons when they attacked. They walked in silence for the remainder of the night. By morning they found themselves far from the border town where they had crossed paths with Kurad, the king's protector.

As the sun rose through the haze they found a quiet glade to rest Samuel's legs for the day. The young king, still straddling the line between the ghost realm and the living, was prone to a fatigue with which the others weren't burdened. Dungarvan used his time to reach out to Tiberius through the amulet to find out if his agent had reached the army of ghosts yet, the news back both encouraging and disappointing.

He soon called for Rathlin to get Samuel on his feet and ready to travel. There were things he needed to confirm and could only be trusted to happen if he stood before them in person.

"He claims to not have the energy to walk. Why not give the boy some more of that potion?"

"It was no more a potion to keep him alive in both worlds than to keep him quiet. Do you want to carry him again?"

"I will use other means."

"Good, there will be a time for its use later and my supply is limited."

It was clear that Samuel had received another dose of Rathlin's anger by the time they showed up ready to travel. Dungarvan didn't ask any questions nor did he hesitate a moment more before they were once again on the trail to meet up with Tiberius.

Three days later, walking through the night and the hazy days between, they finally arrived within sight of the walls of Pendar. Dungarvan had to smile inwardly as he surveyed the work his son had done to lay the city in ruins, the destruction of the dragon still impressive even in this ghostly realm of shadows.

His arrival overdue, he was quick to send Tiberias a summons so that they could connect and discuss the situation his go between had raised the alarm over. Upon seeing his approach from within the city he stepped out of the forest and revealed himself to the man.

"Master, I'm so glad to see you. The army has news you need to hear."

"That's what you told me in our session. I'm here now, what is it?"

"They encountered a man within the city and even engaged in a skirmish with him. Though he escaped they pursued him for a number of days before he got too far from the city and they broke off to return."

"I'm sorry, I don't see the importance of this message."

"He was the same one who came to the inn where we met, I'm sure of it."

"Then he knows I have an army here, and it won't take long for him to connect the cry for help from the boy. The time is not right yet, but I don't think we have a choice except to launch the final offensive against the forces that hold the city. Bring me to their leader, there are a few details I want them to be clear about."

"He is on his way." Tiberias turned to look behind him, his gaze directing Dungarvan towards the assembly that was closing the gap to where they stood at the edge of the forest.

"So he once again rose to the top." He stepped past the man as the leader of the ghost army came to a stop a short distance from the wizard. "Orgle, it's good to see you." Dungarvan paused to smirk, "in one piece."

The Ghosts of Pendar

CHAPTER TWENTY ONE

"Are you okay, Isabel?" The voice came to her as she struggled to shake the cobwebs from her head, though she quickly figured out the haze was really an attribute of where she found herself, not weakness. Kurad reached an accompanying hand down with his question, offering to help her to her feet.

"How is Relysis?" Isabel asked as she looked about, her eyes locking on the three bodies on the floor. The bodies, of course, were their own and to see them slumped to the floor in awkward positions was unnerving.

"He is already out in the hall looking around."

"Where are we?" Isabel forced herself to look away from her own form.

"Still in Drogheda, yet definitely not where we were just moments ago."

"Why is the air so thick? I feel like I need to continually try to rub my eyes. Is it the same for you?"

"More at the periphery."

"Elf eyes. If only I had your blood in my veins rather than dwarven blood."

"Not another word, young lady." Relysis stepped back through the door. "I would hate to have you regretting such a foolish statement."

Isabel did as she was told, though she gave Kurad a sideways glance that intimated her true opinion.

"Are you both ready to go?"

"So this ghost version of the Drogheda is the same?"

"As far as I can tell, just without most of the inhabitants."

"Did you see a ghost? What did it look like?"

"The same as we do. It appeared to be in a hurry and didn't acknowledge me so I think it must have been distracted with something else."

Isabel's interest was piqued at the prospect. The theory they had discussed included the likelihood, and even imperative, to catch up to Samuel and Tralee in this alternate realm. Coming across other individuals hadn't crossed her mind.

"Follow me, we'll try to take the most direct route to the Western Door. From there we'll go cross country and arrive in Pendar in hopes that we can catch up to Samuel before he gets there."

"He is many days ahead of us and was nearly to Pendar when I crossed paths with him."

"We will need to move fast then," Relysis stated as he led them from his room.

Isabel had to hurry to catch up, the general exhibiting a burst of speed that belied his size. Looking about she stepped outside the room, half expecting to find her father waiting for her, but knowing he couldn't be as it had been decided he would stay beyond the room for this very reason. The disappointment was still the same.

Relysis wasn't slowing down, and Kurad was guiding her to follow in the general's wake lest they get left behind. It didn't take more than a nudge to get Isabel focused and moving. Before he turned another corner they caught up to their guide and were pushing him to go faster as they wound their way through the maze of tunnels that crisscrossed deep within the mountain.

"Is anyone else thirsty? Do ghosts need to drink?" Isabel asked when they stopped to rest their legs.

"I don't feel like they would need to, their physical bodies aren't here with them." Kurad opined though there was an uncertainty on his face as though he questioned himself.

"Then we are dependent on the healer and his staff to make sure our bodies are replenished." Isabel took Kurad's response to be true and expanded on it. Relysis agreed.

"They have been taking care of Samuel and Tralee this whole time. As long as your father gets us to the hospital ward we won't falter here."

"I'm glad we left him behind then." Isabel still felt conflicted about suggesting he couldn't come along, however, this new revelation left her feeling better.

"Come now, Relysis, we need to get going. We are still days from where I heard Samuel's ghost call my name."

"I hope they feed me soon," Relysis said with a wry grin behind his beard. He got to his feet and quickly headed off down the tunnel leaving the other two to once again scramble to catch up.

They traversed many miles of tunnels and halls before they came to an intersection where the general had to stop, tugging on his beard trying to figure out which way he wanted to go. Isabel took the opportunity to find a spot to sit by Kurad, steeling herself for the conversation she had refrained from starting until now.

"When you went to Pendar, was it as bad as I've been told? I mean is there any chance to rebuild?"

"It would be a massive undertaking even for an army of strong backed dwarves."

"So you're saying I should not be ruling it out then?"

"Pendar had its place in your country's history, but with the trolls revealing new veins of ore to the dwarves there is more potential in the mountain than ever before."

"So even in the ghost world you're not going to let me have my dreams of living above ground."

"Sorry."

"Tell me then about these ghosts you say have moved into the city. How were they able to attack you?"

"I haven't figured that out yet, though my hunch now that we know Dungarvan has reached out from the grave to influence the living, is that he is behind this."

"Why Pendar though? You said yourself that it is not worth rebuilding. What purpose would drive him to have an army of ghosts within the walls?"

"If we figure that out we will be a lot closer to solving this puzzle. It looks like Relysis has figured out the way to go from here. We best be moving, he seems to have extra energy now that he's a ghost."

"His old joints probably don't hurt so much in this realm."

"I heard that, young lady," Relysis barked over his shoulder at Isabel garnering a laugh from both Kurad and Isabel that eventually caught Relysis too until he turned and put a finger to his lips, abruptly cutting off the laughter.

"What is it?" Kurad whispered, creeping forward to stand next to the general.

"Voices ahead in the tunnel. I can't make them out though."

"Could it be Samuel?" Isabel asked as she inched forward to make sure she didn't miss anything.

"Not unless the wizard brought him back here, but with the army of ghosts in Pendar I can't believe returning here would be their objective."

"Then who do you think?" Relysis asked, turning to Kurad as if he were the expert on ghosts among the three of them.

"I'm sure many lives were lost within these halls over the years it served as homeland to the dwarves. If it isn't the wizard we seek you may be about to meet long lost ancestors of yours."

"I hadn't thought of that."

"Me either," Isabel was quick to add, a concerned look readily apparent on her face as she asked about her greatest fear . "What about non-dwarves? Could the dagar be haunting these halls too."

"I'm not sure," Kurad replied.

"Unless it learned to speak the common tongue of Dulin I think we're safe." Relysis' answer helped Isabel ease her tension just a hair. "I suggest we shadow them for awhile. They seem to be going the same direction as we are."

All of them agreed to the general's plan and they set out trying to maintain a safe distance behind the voices that carried to them, while making sure they made no unnecessary sounds to give those they were trailing cause to raise the alarm. Unfortunately they were not as good at it as they thought, rounding a corner they were confronted by a squad of hammer bearing ghosts who weren't intimated by the three of them.

"Drop your axe and you your sword." The commands came swiftly as the ghosts before them raised their own weapons. "And you in the back, know that you won't get an arrow notched before we disable you."

Isabel knew that they weren't to be trifled with and stepped back out from behind Kurad, reaching her bow from her back, and placing it on the ground along with her companions' weapons. Standing back up she shifted nervously as their captors shouted down the tunnel, receiving an unsettling response from a chorus of voices.

Soon the tunnel before her was filled with dwarves that looked like they had been ghosts forever, their beards and leathers covered in dust from ages long past. Their questions all blurred together and were indistinguishable, they all spoke over one another until one voice cut through the noise as a familiar face emerged from the crowd.

"Bruff, tell your squad to put their weapons down, all of them. This is General Relysis Halfthor, Kurad the king's protector, and Isabel, Princess of Pendar."

"Mayor Tralee, it is so good to see you," Relysis stated, "We hoped we would find you."

"Halfthor?" Bruff asked as he stepped forward next to Tralee. "That name has a familiar sound. I had a friend when

I was just a lad who joined the army the same time I joined the miners."

"It is an honor to meet you, Bruff. My family has been members of the army for generations and to get to speak with someone who knew an ancestor is quite an honor."

"And Isabel, the mayor tells me that you are a hero of Drogheda. Was is that very bow that you used to slay the dagar?"

Isabel was caught off guard by the familiarity with which this ghost dwarf spoke of her story, she had to gather her thoughts for a moment before she replied. "I don't feel like a hero. I just did what I could do in that moment."

"Then you should retrieve your weapons, all of you, for we march to save your brother from the wizards who hold him and we will likely need your skills before this is over."

"You have seen him? Is he okay?"

"He was the last we saw him. It's been awhile though," Bruff answered.

"They are heading to Pendar," Kurad interjected.

"We had heard the same, but why Pendar?" Tralee asked, his confusion evident on his face.

"Dungarvan has an army of ghosts waiting for him there."

"Then it is good that we have a general to lead this ragtag group of miners now." Bruff paused before adding for all of his crew to hear, "It's time to leave the mountain boys, we march for Pendar."

CHAPTER TWENTY TWO

"Is my army ready to take the castle?"

"We were told you were coming only a day ago."

"You've had more than enough time to finally complete this task, or will I need to step in and take control?"

"I was under the impression you had another dragon with you. Are you hiding that one too until you are ready?"

Dungarvan looked past the gnome posturing for his escort's benefit. Resisting the urge to transition into his own dragon and obliterate the gnome with enough dragon fire that even his spirit wouldn't survive, he took a deep breath to clear his head. He couldn't help but smile when he saw the gnome usurper flinch when he exhaled without an accompanying explosion of fire.

"There will be a time when I call for dragon's fire but not today."

"We have pushed the dwarves back to the castle grounds. They need only another serious offensive, one that you and the other dragon can provide, and it will be mine once again."

"You can do what you will with what remains of the city once I have claimed what I have come here for."

"How do you know the book is still in the castle?"

"There is nothing else they have left to them in this world. It is the only reason they cling to the castle and this shadow of their former lives. I'm going to give them a reason to hand it to me willingly."

"We have quarters prepared for you and those who travel with you, they should be perfect for you and your dragons."

Dungarvan saw through the intent of the gnome's statement. There were a few secrets he had maintained for this moment and he wasn't ready yet to let Orgle in on the last of the details. If the elder Samuel knew his grandson was to be the bait in this trap there could be a shift in the dynamics and all would be lost. He couldn't know until the last moment.

"Lead the way, I will summon them once I know we are safe to enter."

Orgle barked orders to his soldiers and they quickly fanned out before them as they led the wizard in through what remained of the city gates. As he looked about at the ruins up close he realized the power of a dragon in flight. If only either of them could achieve that in this ghostly realm it would assure him of the victory he craved, however, the ability was seemingly lost to them both. It was something he would need to press Rathlin on over the next few days as they made the final battle preparations.

Turning his focus back to the city, he walked amongst the rubble of the buildings and could sense the soldiers in his army lurking in the shadows. They were all very careful to stay back from the doorways and windows lest he spot them. It spoke of their fear of him even in this ghostly realm. His reputation clearly had preceded him. He let them hide, for now.

Orgle followed a trail that only he knew, and it seemed for a while the gnome leader was trying to disorient Dungarvan until they finally arrived at the remnants of a building that had been given to the wizard for his headquarters.

"I hope it is to your liking. There aren't any buildings left intact since your son razed the city."

"So were you aware of the happenings?"

"Not exactly. Buildings began to crumble about us and there was a sense of the dragon's power that reverberated across the chasm between the living and the dead. It wasn't until new soldiers, some we have since recruited into our army, began arriving did we get a full accounting."

"It's interesting that they were receptive to staying and helping you."

"The allure of bringing them back to the living held great sway over them. That offer still stands for us all, doesn't it?"

"There will be choices that will need to be made," Dungarvan answered somewhat vaguely before adding, "I will remember those key to the victory." Orgle's smile showed that he was convinced that he would be rewarded and at the moment that was all Dungarvan needed.

"I need to call my men to me." His statement was an effective dismissal and Orgle, who was keen to make the wizard understand his importance, needed no more instruction to disappear. With the use of the dragon's claw amulet he gave Tiberias instructions to bring Rathlin, Samuel, and his pet gnome to him using his matching amulet as a location beacon.

His headquarters were in a wide open building, the walls and most of the roof gone. With the space, and some time to himself, he decided it was a perfect opportunity to test the spell he needed his son to master also. He had spent all the years he been trapped within this realm trying to make it work to no avail. There was something different about the air in this ghostly world that wouldn't let him take flight as the dragon and he hadn't puzzled it out yet.

With the battle looming, time was against him and he knew that. That added pressure would either chase away any possibility of finally recognizing the change he needed to make to the words and achieving flight, or his desperation would galvanize his mind and that which had been elusive for all this time would be suddenly found. He hoped for the latter as he mulled the spell over in this mind once again, yet he felt resigned that it maybe the former.

Reciting the words once again he felt the transformation begin. His body grew larger, his skin grew thicker, and his vision began to change to the reptilian nature of the beast he was becoming. The wizard waited patiently for the final moments to pass, unwilling to rush the process in fear of disrupting the successful completion, before stretching his wings to test them.

Looking about to make sure he had enough room for his enormous wing span, he tentatively stretched them out to their full splendor. Turning his head he stared at them in awe. They nearly spanned the entire building Orgle had provided him and the dragon skin nearly glowed in the ghostly light. Pumping them carefully he could feel the strength that they exuded with each up and down motion, and that is what left him perplexed about not being able to take flight. Everything pointed to him being able to take off and soar except the air itself wouldn't support him.

"Father, I can see it now!"

Rathlin's voice cut through his concentration and he slowly turned his massive dragon head to stare at the diminutive figures standing off to the side. His son stepped away from the others. The dragon spell on his lips, he began to walk towards Dungarvan, growing with every step as the transformation began. Soon Rathlin was nearly as large as himself and the two beasts had to jostle for space within the building, but not for long. Rathlin spread his wings, pumped them several times, and launched himself into the night sky.

Dungarvan watched his son from below, his chest filling with pride, as his son circled several times over the city he had destroyed in life. Unable to contain it any longer Dungarvan pointed his dragon's mouth straight up and let out a thunderous gout of flames that shook the buildings about him. Then watched as Rathlin matched his fire and swooped down low over the castle, lighting up the sky for all to see his splendor.

The boy had recognized the change they needed to make to the spell for them to take flight in the ghostly realm they existed in for now. This development changed everything he had planned for the upcoming battle. There was nothing the ghost king and his army of dwarves could do to withstand two dragons in flight with their flames laying everything about them to waste. The thought brought another rush of flames from deep within him that once again shook the ground.

Quickly making the required adjustment to the spell before he launched himself into the air to fly alongside his son, the pair lit up the night sky for all below to see. His army would be emboldened at the sight and the dwarves of Pendar would be running for their holes. The battle was over before it had even begun.

The Ghosts of Pendar

CHAPTER TWENTY THREE

"Dragons!" The shouts rang out into the night as the guards manning the castle outposts sounded the alarm. The chorus of voices was quickly joined by the soldiers who formed the defensive ring closer to the castle grounds. In no time the troops in the barracks rushed out to see the spectacle for themselves, for at no time in their ghostly existence had they seen a dragon in flight.

"Everyone to their battle stations. The wizard is back and his attack is imminent." At Samuel's word dispatches were sent to all the commanders, though they were certainly already preparing for the rush of soldiers sure to accompany the fire breathing beasts soaring above the city.

"How will we hold the city against a pair of dragons? They will rain fire down on us from above. Are we to huddle below our shields and hope the dwarven steel will save us?"

"It wasn't what I envisioned, but if we have to we will until we come up with another plan. Dwarven steel has kept the wizard's army at bay for all this time. I don't see that we should start doubting its effectiveness now."

"I guess that's why you are the king, my brother. I have never had the confidence you possess."

"Don't sell yourself short, Stephen. You stayed behind with me instead of going on to the halls of our ancestors for a reason."

"You give me credit that seems unwarranted. I only stayed to try and avenge your wife's murder because I failed to protect her in life, and I have not yet been successful."

"I don't hold you responsible and I'm sure when we finally get to go to the halls of Dagda she will be there waiting to greet you and tell you the same thing."

"Let's get this over with so we can both do just that. We've been here too long already."

"I agree. Let's get down to the front lines and see what we have to contend with tonight."

The brothers made their way quickly down to where the commanders of Samuel's army were barking orders to the soldiers to take up their positions.

"Have you seen any advance from the wizard's army?" Samuel asked the first commander he encountered.

"Nothing of any substance. A small force charged our lines as the dragons circled above, but the dragons offered them no support and the word from our boys is that we quickly threw them back."

"Then the dragons were merely for show tonight. Their hope was to sow fear amongst us before the main attack. Be on the ready, it may come at any time."

Samuel looked skyward to see if the beasts were back in the air. This new development with the dragons was going to change the complexity of the upcoming battle. They had no provision in their arsenal to contend with an attack from the sky. To find the answer he knew he must find one of the newest members of his army, one who had suffered the defeat of Pendar and who would know what happened first hand. He knew where a handful of those men were stationed along the wall and headed that way.

Stopping along the way to talk with his soldiers he got a more complete account of the feints the wizard's army of gnomes and trolls had conducted. When putting all the separate details together it confirmed his initial impression that they had not been coordinated with the appearance of the dragons, rather an opportunistic commander who hoped to take advantage of the distraction.

He was proud of his boys not to let the dragons completely capture their attention and allow their lines to be breached. More than once the defensive ring had been penetrated and every time it happened they had been forced to fall back to reestablish their perimeter. It was why they clung now to the castle and the walls surrounding it. They couldn't afford to lose anymore ground and still expect to protect the book from being captured. For now it was safe and as he approached the men he had been looking for he pushed his concern aside.

"I'm looking for someone who was in the city when the dragon attacked."

"We all were, Your Highness."

"Not just now," Samuel clarified as he looked around at the large group who stood along the broken wall. "I meant when the city fell in the land of the living."

"That would be the whole of our group."

It took Samuel a moment to realize the enormity of the loss to have so many in his ranks from that one battle. "No wonder the city was lost to the beast and his army."

"We brought him down, but by then it was too late. The city had been destroyed and there was nothing left to do except to get clear and fight another day. Unfortunately, those who survived the dragon still had to deal with his army."

"Though it may not have seemed good at the time, mayhap it is a good thing that you are here now. I need to know how you brought down the dragon last time."

"That we can do. General Halfthor went to work."

Samuel interrupted the man upon hearing his trusted general's name. "Wait, Relysis still walks among the living?"

"He did the last time any of us saw him."

"So what did that old dwarf come up with to battle the dragon?"

"We built large bows to fling giant arrows at the beast as he flew past us."

"And this worked?"

"It destroyed all of the bows until there was only one left. Rumor has it the half-elf Kurad took it down in the end, though I was no longer there to see it."

"I would have very much liked to see that too so I understand your disappointment. Though you name him the same as my dear friend, I wonder if he is the same. I did not know of any elven heritage."

"I can't speak to it other than his father was elven royalty."

"So Kurad found his family. There isn't much in this realm to find comfort, but I will hold tight to this revelation. Thank you." Samuel gripped the man's shoulder tightly as he let the emotion flow freely, an urge to smile he hadn't felt for too long coming over him. "I sure miss him, though I don't wish that he were here with me now. Those living in Pendar need him more than I. Could you tell me who the king is?" Samuel's question was never answered as the call came from the front lines.

"Gnomes coming fast and hard!"

Shouts from a short distance away interrupted Samuel's discussion and he pulled his sword free to look skyward for any sign of the dragons he was convinced would accompany all future attacks. Seeing an empty sky above, he raced away from the men and towards the calls for reinforcements.

By the time he got there the ghostly gnomes had crossed the short distance that separated the lines of the two forces and were nearly upon the dwarves who were bracing for the impact behind their wall of shields. Men with bows stood behind them, balancing on any structure still standing that was tall enough for them to see above the fray, and letting their dwarven steel tipped arrows fly into the oncoming mass.

The arrows sliced through the throng coming at them, gnomes evaporating into nothingness as the dwarven steel pierced them. But there were only so many archers. Many more gnomes survived the hail of arrows than fell and they crashed against the dwarves' shield wall with greater numbers than the dwarves possessed. Gritting their teeth and holding tight to their shields, they bore the weight of the gnome attackers as long as they possibly could before the first crack in the wall became a flood of gnome soldiers breaking loose inside the dwarven ranks.

Battleaxes replaced shields in the hands of the dwarves as they tried to turn the gnome army back and to force them to retreat through the same fissure they had broke through. Samuel raced to that very spot and forced his way through the fierce dwarves who were begrudgingly giving up as little ground as they could.

Standing above his shorter dwarven warriors, he had the first opportunity to see the pair of trolls who were following in the wake of the gnome attack and called out to those around him.

"Rally to me boys, we have trolls joining the fun tonight." At his order any dwarf not engaged in fierce battle raced to stand with their king. Even before his squad had formed up completely he began to push forward, as eager to bring the fight to the trolls as they were relishing matching up against the ghost king of Pendar.

The gnomes scattered before him, all too willing to get clear of the giant of a man with the great broadsword who was marching through them as if they didn't exist. Only the random swipe cleaved any who had thoughts of glory and they quickly dissipated into the haze.

"You've come to try again tonight. I thought you would have learned your lesson every night for the last fifty years." Samuel knew how this would go, the trolls never changed their tactics no matter how badly they lost. He would cut them down and then they would dissipate into the night only to come together again the next. Their death in the land of the dead was temporary, needing only a day to re-form and come at him again the next night. He believed tonight would be no different, but tonight he was wrong.

The fireball coming straight at him from high in the sky was his only warning that the battlefield had shifted in favor of the wizard's army.

The Ghosts of Pendar

CHAPTER TWENTY FOUR

"How long before we reach the Western Door?" Isabel asked as she fell back in the line to talk to the general.

"We should be there before the sun rises."

"I'm not a dwarf. That means absolutely nothing to me."

"Sorry, I forget sometimes. If time moves the same on this side of death as it did when we walked among the living then dawn is just a couple hours past."

"Thank you, that's much better. I have a question for you. Are you having as hard of a time keeping up with our ghostly escort as I am?"

"Now that you ask, my legs have grown increasingly tired with every mile we walk. Yesterday wasn't nearly as exhausting as today."

"I haven't asked him, but Kurad seems to not be his usual self either."

"What are you thinking? You seem pretty perceptive for one so young."

"Keep track of how you're feeling and we'll compare tonight when we stop to rest. Have you seen the mayor, I want to talk with him too."

Relysis shrugged his broad shoulders and scanned up and down the line of dwarves that coursed along the tunnels deep within the mountain.

"That's okay, I'll find him soon enough." She stepped out of the line and let those they were traveling with stream by until she finally saw the mayor coming along the walkway. Waiting until he got alongside her she stepped back in the line, startling the mayor who seemed to be lost in his thoughts.

"Sorry, Mayor Tralee, I didn't mean to disrupt you."

"Oh no, Princess Isabel. I never mind helping you with anything you need."

"You're too kind. I was wondering how you are getting along in this realm?"

"The company seems alright, now that they don't think I'm an agent of the wizard. That was a little tense, to be certain."

"Yes, they seem an honorable group of dwarves. That's not what I meant though. I was really wanting to know how you feel. Your energy levels with all this walking, how are holding up?"

"I feel actually quite good. I'm not used to this much physical activity in the course of my duties, however, it seems like I've adjusted to the rigors just fine. In fact, I have even been thinking when we get back that I might need to get out and explore more of the tunnels."

"That's interesting. My own experience hasn't been the same. I would rather sit down and take a nap."

"Indeed that is strange, back in your body you are full of energy."

"Relysis is experiencing the same fatigue. I'm starting to wonder if something is wrong. Have you seen Kurad? I would like to talk with him before I rush to any decision."

"I'm near the tail end of our caravan and I haven't seen him since our last rest stop. I would look up front."

"I was afraid you were going to say that." Isabel offered a weak smile to the mayor before she forced herself to increase her pace and began to move up through those she had just let pass her by waiting for Mayor Tralee.

Even as she felt she was walking as fast as she could, she was barely passing any of the dwarves in the line. She attempted to pick up her pace by transitioning into a trot, but her feet felt like they were encased in the same granite of the mountain. Fighting against the weight that dragged at her legs seemed to only make it worse and she quickly fell back to a walk.

For the next hour she had to be content with just keeping her place in line. However, soon after, she began slipping back with dwarves passing her regularly until she was once again trudging alongside the mayor.

"Did you get to talk to Kurad?"

"No, I never made it up to him." Isabel replied between gasps for air.

"Princess, are you alright?"

"I don't know, I just can't seem to get my breath and my legs are like stone."

"I'll get help, you just sit tight." Tralee guided her to a spot along the wall that had a rock for her to sit. "You two watch over her, I'm going to get Kurad and Relysis."

Isabel could hear the mayor calling out for Kurad and Relysis as he disappeared up the tunnel in search of her companions. His voice seemed to fade out before long as did those of the ghost dwarves that stood nearby to keep an eye on her. Squinting her eyes it seemed as if their lips were moving, but she heard nothing of what they said. Cocking her head she leaned forward and strained to hear what they were saying when suddenly spots began to swirl at the periphery of her vision and she quietly pitched forward to the floor.

"She's back here, just a little further."

"Slow down, I can't keep up," Relysis grumbled to Tralee's surprise.

"We're almost there. How are you doing Kurad?"

"I'm winded too, and my legs are heavy."

"It's the same as Isabel described."

By the time the mayor arrived back where he had left Isabel with Relysis and Kurad in tow the dwarves had rolled her over and were doing their best to revive her with no avail.

"What happened here?" Tralee barked when he saw the princess laying prone on the floor of the tunnel.

"She had a curious look on her face, didn't say a word, and then just tipped over," one of the dwarves answered, the dumfounded look on his face matching his voice.

"Let's get these two a seat also, they look like she did when I left her here to rest." Tralee turned his two charges over to the dwarves to help get them settled before he turned his attention to the princess laying on the floor. After a quick check he got back to his feet and went back to Kurad and Relysis.

"She's still breathing, but her heart is weak, and honestly you two don't seem much better."

"You feel fine though?" Kurad asked.

"Yes, and so do all the others. It's just you three that are suffering from this curious fatigue." Tralee said.

"Something must be wrong back in Drogheda. I mean with our bodies. I know that your body is being tended to by the healers so that is why you are doing fine even after being here longer than us. We expected ours to be taken care of likewise, we even left King Edward to make certain of it," Relysis stated.

"I feel there is something wrong, we need to get you back there immediately." Kurad stated as he gave Relysis a knowing look.

"It's going to have to be you. Kurad and I are in no condition to go running back to our bodies, we're soon to be sprawled out on the floor just as the princess is right now."

The mayor saw the truth of what the general said, he was the only one who could get back to the living and bring them aid.

"Where were you when you read the book?"

"My quarters, but be careful. If something happened to Edward then there might be more to this than we realize."

"I will do what I can to save you." Tralee knew that time was against him so he said quick goodbyes to the ghosts he had gotten to know and was soon running along the ancient paths through the mountain.

The hours went by and Tralee kept pushing himself to run without stopping, almost reveling in the fact that as a ghost he was no longer encumbered by the rigors of old age, his joints no longer aching as they did when he was alive. There was one thing, however, that he knew he would relish upon his return to his body and that was to take a long draw from an oversized mug of ale. He had never known such thirst in all his days.

Using that motivation he continued to run long into the night and even into the day beyond. Coursing through the tunnels he chose unerringly at each intersection he came upon, confident in his memory of the ancient hallways that he had been so enthralled with as they marched towards the Western Door. Soon he could hear the falls ahead of him and knew that his journey was almost done, he could only hope that his efforts would save his three companions teetering on the brink of actually dying.

Running out onto the great bridge he only slowed when a dark figure stepped out from behind one of the giant dwarf statues that lined the length of the span. His instincts screamed at him to turn and run back the other way, the man's aura spoke nothing but danger to Tralee. Forcing himself forward at a much slower pace he got within earshot of the shadowy figure, finally stopping as the man spoke.

"I knew someone would come to try and rescue them. I just didn't imagine it would be you," The man said as a blade appeared suddenly in his hand, punctuating the motion with a low whistle.

"Who are you? You shouldn't be down here."

"Turns out I'm exactly where I need to be. I can't let you get the help they need to keep their bodies alive. There is little time left for those who fell to the spell, and I have already killed the old king. You've already failed."

"I need you to let me pass. If I'm already too late it won't matter."

"Sorry, I can't allow that. I need to make sure my task is complete before I return to report to my master."

Tralee knew what he must do and he stepped haltingly forward as his legs refused to do his bidding. The man before had no such misgivings and began to stride forward towards the mayor, a glint in his eyes that told Tralee he was familiar with his trade of dealing out death. Tralee's mind raced as he tried to figure out how he could possibly avoid the fate that approached him when he caught a movement from behind the man.

Squinting into the haze he realized who it was, his smile that matched the assassin's didn't go unnoticed and the man turned to look behind him to see the ghost of Edward stalking towards him with his giant battleaxe held before him.

"I have been waiting for you too."

"So you want me to kill you again?"

"In life I was carrying the wounds from a treacherous attack, those no longer encumber me."

Tralee watched as the man shrunk back from the king, circling to stay out of reach of the battleaxe as he tried to find an opening in Edward's defenses. Edward didn't give him any opportunities and soon had the man scrambling to stay away from the sharp blade that swished past him, growing closer with each pass until the man stumbled and felt the full force of Edward's wrath that nearly cut the man in half. Standing over the body, Edward reached down and plucked the dragon's claw amulet from the man's neck and held it up for Tralee to see.

"This is what allowed him to pass between the living and the dead. Unfortunately for him, it offered no protection in life against my blade in the ghost realm. Do you know where the others are?"

"They are on their way to Pendar, Dungarvan has Samuel and they are going there."

"Hurry now, you must get back to the healer so he can save those who are still in Relysis' quarters."

"Come with me. Maybe it's not too late to save you too."

"My time amongst the living is over, but don't worry, my work isn't done yet and I won't abandon my people. Go now, run!"

Tralee had no choice but to do his king's bidding as he raced across the bridge faster than he could ever remember running. Never slowing, he was at the healer's quarters in what seemed like a blink in time. Skidding to a halt as he came into the room, he looked at his own body lying peacefully on the bed. He would have like to spend a moment more to take it all in one last time, but knew there wasn't the time available for that indulgence.

Without even thinking how the process would work, he dove headfirst back into his body. The sensation of his spirit rejoining his physical body had his head swirling for long moments as he wondered if it was going to work. Then, suddenly, he was back and his eyes popped open as he gasped for air. Clumsily pushing himself up from the bed, he called urgently for help and a healer immediately came running across the room.

"Isabel, Kurad and Relysis are in the general's quarters, they need your help immediately, I'll explain later. Just go now!" Tralee watched as the healer ran back out of the room calling for help and several of them rushed away down the hall towards Relysis' room.

The exhaustion of the last several days caught up to him then and he let himself flop back down onto the bed. He could only hope that they arrived in time to save the three, but the tears began to flow when the full weight of losing Edward struck him. Tralee knew he was okay in the ghost realm, but didn't know how he was going to explain that to anyone. The loss of the old king to those in the land of the living would reverberate throughout the entire kingdom.

The Ghosts of Pendar

CHAPTER TWENTY FIVE

"Your Highness, the mayor is awake."

Jessica couldn't believe her ears when the attendant rushed into her room. It took her a moment to gather herself from her reverie before she got up from her chair by the fire and followed her from the room. On the way to the hospital ward she had a flood of questions coursing through her mind, but understandably the first that escaped her lips concerned her son.

"Is Samuel awake too, he's been gone longer."

"I'm sorry, they did not say, Your Highness. We will have to wait to find out when we get there."

Jessica nodded and increased their pace as much as they could within the crowded corridors in that area of the city. The same rumor that reached her own ears had spread quickly amongst the inhabitants and their natural inclination was to seek confirmation for themselves.

Her frustration was building when suddenly a squad of dwarves wearing the home guard's insignia appeared from the crowd and formed a protective ring around the queen and rushed her to the hospital ward. Arriving in the room they spread out along the wall and cleared a path for Jessica to step inside and go directly to the mayor's bed where she reached out and took his hand in hers.

"Tralee, I didn't know that I would ever speak to you again. It seems a miracle that you have come back to us."

"Samuel is still there, and so are Relysis, Kurad, and the princess Isabel."

"I only meant that you were in a deep sleep. Where is there, and how do you even know that they are away? They have been gone now for a few days, but we do not believe they have left Drogheda."

"It's much more complicated than that."

Shouts from the doorway prevented the two of them from continuing their conversation. Healers ran alongside those who carried four stretchers into the room, the first three transporting, Isabel, Kurad, and Relysis, but the fourth was covered with a sheet to conceal the identity of whomever that individual was.

"Isabel!" Jessica shrieked when she saw her daughter.

"Give them space, they know what they are doing." Tralee explained, trying to protect the queen from what he knew was coming.

"She's alive, if barely. We need to get her fluids like we did with the mayor and Samuel. They are all very weak." One of the healers explained while they scurried about getting their new patients settled in.

"What about this other one?"

"Jessica, don't go." Tralee tried to hold her hand tightly.

Jessica shook her hand free and walked towards the last strctcher that had entered the room. The healers were rushing about attending to the other three and barely took note of the queen as she walked across the room and finally stood before the last individual. In her mind she tried to deny who it was, but there had been only one other person who had gone with the other three and still she reached out to pull the sheet back.

"Your Highness please, you don't have to."

The voice came from her elbow as a hand grabbed her own and stopped her from pulling the cover free. In that moment she looked about and realized the home guard had all assembled across from her, their hoods pulled up over their heads as they looked down at the floor.

Turning to the dwarf holding her hand firm she noted the tears streaming down his cheeks to disappear within his thick beard. It was the only confirmation she needed and she collapsed onto Edward's body, the sobs wracking her body as she clutched him to her. She could feel his familiar form beneath the sheet and, in anger, yanked away the thin barrier that kept them apart. Her tears continued to flow as she collapsed atop him and buried her face in his chest.

Jessica didn't know how long she clung to Edward before another pair of hands encouraged her to let go of him. She had nothing left in her to fight their guidance and stood up from where she had been kneeling next to his bed. Looking down at him through bloodshot eyes she saw for the first time the dried blood surrounding his wound.

"Who did this to him? I want them found so I can pay them back for this."

"Edward already has exacted his revenge. His killer has been dealt with."

"How do you know this?" Jessica didn't mean to sound accusatory, but her response to the mayor's statement was harsh all the same.

"Like I said, it's very complicated. You're going to need to come and sit so I can tell you about a realm that exists just outside our own. One that is often spoken of though none of us had any idea of whether it really existed. It is the realm of those who have gone before us in death, and it's filled with nearly as much life as we know here among the living."

"I'm going to need to hear this too." Willos stood in the entryway to the healers' ward. News of King Edward's death reached every corner of Drogheda faster than the messenger carrying it could run.

"Willos, you will need to have the Guardians go down to the Galway Bridge. They will find the one who killed Edward there."

"Edward was found in Relysis' quarters, how could he be there? He would have had to been injured and collapsed there. How do you know all of this, didn't you just wake up?"

"You have strung together a raft of questions for me. It seems before I can go back to the beginning of my adventure that I must start at the end and work my way backwards." Tralee repositioned himself so he was sitting on the edge of his bed, his strength returning with every moment his spirit was back in his body.

"I came upon the bridge and was confronted by the assassin who had killed Edward in the general's quarters. His mission was to stop me from returning my spirit to my body which would have meant the death of the three currently being attended by the healers. It was while I was trying to figure out how to evade him that Edward, or rather his ghost, arrived on the bridge and with that giant battleaxe of his he cleaved the man in half."

"That's impossible, he wasn't able to do that with his injuries." Willos was unconvinced of the mayor's account.

"It's true, I tell you. His body is no longer limited by the injury he suffered in life, it was as if he was reborn with his former strength."

"You mean he still lives there? Can you bring him back to me like you did?"

"I'm sorry, Your Highness, I truly am, but I was there by way of the wizard's book of spells just like Samuel and now Isabel, Relysis, and Kurad. King Edward came to be there as a result of his death in this realm."

"You knew his fate before you came back here?"

"I spoke with him after he had slain the assassin about what was happening with Samuel and Isabel."

Jessica had to inhale deeply to keep the tears from coming forth once more. The mayor's account wasn't what she wanted to hear and she desperately needed a distraction.

"The rest of them, my children, can be brought back to me at any time?"

"The princess, Relysis, and Kurad were under duress when I left. Luckily we figured out that their bodies weren't being attended to like Samuel and I. That's why I came back here. If I hadn't there would be three more bodies to mourn over."

"What do we have to do to wake them up?"

"We have to wait for them to finish what they went there to do. The three who are hopefully recovering now need to rescue Samuel."

"Rescue him from what?"

"From whom, I'm afraid. The ghosts of the wizard Dungarvan and his son Rathlin have Samuel with them and they are taking him to Pendar for a reason I don't know, but Kurad spoke of an army of ghosts occupying the city."

"You have my head spinning, I don't know how you speak of all of this and aren't terrified."

"They are in good company, I assure you. They have joined with a group of miners lost in the depths of Drogheda thousands of years ago, and they are heading to Pendar right now."

Jessica continued to try to understand the reality of what the mayor spoke so calmly about. She was about to inquire if this could have all been a dream when a guardian arrived at the door and announced the assassin had been found exactly where Tralee said he would be, and that he had died in the manner described.

"Is there anything we can do for them here?"

"We need to keep them nourished, that is the key for them to be able to exist there."

"Can we send an army there too?" Willos spoke up again after silently listening to the story.

"I don't know that you could send an army of the living to impact the outcome of whatever battle is coming in the realm of the ghosts."

"Edward will help my children return to me. There has to be a purpose. His death will not be wasted, he will make sure of that."

The Ghosts of Pendar

CHAPTER TWENTY SIX

"She's coming around. Isabel, can you hear me? Isabel."

Isabel heard the voice calling her name and she instinctively turned toward it as she emerged from the fog that had settled over her causing her to collapse to the floor.

"How long have I been out?"

"Three days, we were beginning to worry about all three of you."

"Where are Kurad and Relysis?"

"They woke up a little while ago they are recovering just up the tunnel."

"Can you take me to them? I have some questions for them."

"Are you steady enough to walk on your own?"

Isabel was confident that she was until she swayed upon standing. A pair of strong hands caught her and held her upright, waiting patiently until she actually was ready to go on under her own power. Nodding to her guardian, she stepped off cautiously with much better results than her first attempt. She wasn't sure if she markedly improved or if the hands she could sense that were ready to catch her should she falter again motivated her to do better.

She was glad that they didn't have to go far before she saw her two companions sitting up with their backs against the cool granite recuperating. "So are you two going to be long?"

"I see at least your wit has recovered, Princess, though your gait tells a slightly different story."

"You have a keen eye, Kurad. I am no more ready to resume our journey than you are, likely less so."

"When you collapsed we determined that our bodies were not being tended by the healers as his was. So we sent Tralee back with all speed that he could muster to sound the alarm.

The mayor must have made it back to the city and alerted someone to come to our aid and now we are recovering."

"Is that what happened? Our bodies went undiscovered? That doesn't make sense though, my father was waiting just outside the room. He wouldn't have left us there."

"I cannot tell you what happened."

"We have no time to return to figure it out ourselves. With Mayor Tralee back amongst the living he will have to solve that mystery."

"I feel stronger with every passing moment, we might as well start our caravan moving again even if we are traveling at less than full speed."

"Kurad is ready to go. Relysis, are you going to let the elf out do you?"

"I liked you better when you were passed out on the floor. If you are asking, of course I'm ready. I was just waiting for you two to get caught up with one another." Relysis hopped to his feet to demonstrate his readiness, but was quick to put out a steadying hand on the wall to keep from toppling.

""Then we have a consensus, we will not push the pace today."

Relysis nodded at Isabel's proclamation as he took a couple deep breaths before tentatively releasing his grip on the wall. They formed up the caravan of ghosts shortly after and, with Bruff in the lead, they resumed their march towards the Western Door.

As expected, the three visitors to the ghostly realm began to regain their strength, and they all agreed to keep pushing forward so they could reach the end of this first leg of their journey before the day ended. So it was with renewed determination, that as the day was coming to a close they arrived at the anteroom to the Western Door where they stopped to regroup and plan the next leg of their travels.

"When was the last time any of you were outside the mountain?" Isabel was sitting down next to Bruff to rest her legs.

"Well, according to Tralee it's been a thousand years or more for us."

"Much will have changed then."

"Trees come and go, as do the villages of the humans, but the mountains grow slowly so I believe that much of it will look familiar. Especially if we were to go back underground and use some of our ancient pathways."

"I know of one," Isabel stated, "but how many are there that would take us towards Pendar?"

"The mountains are riddled with them, and some go so deep you can find the birthplace of the mountains, you just need to know where to look."

"Why would you make underground tunnels when walking above ground would be much faster?"

"If you were planning on making just one trip, then I would agree that your method would be most logical. However, if you intend to make countless trips with supplies and riches dug from the mountains far off, then having a secure underground highway is the better option."

"Who would threaten a dwarven force marching through the mountain passes? It seems to me that the years spent mining would have used valuable resources."

"Back when I was alive there were hoards of orcs running about in the hills. We couldn't hardly come above ground without being harassed for our steel. The army would have been spread thin trying to protect our caravans and there would have been untold losses."

"What would you suggest is our best option to travel quickly on this particular journey?"

"I would say we do as Relysis wishes, he is the general."

"Does he know about these tunnels?"

"Not that I know of, most would have been lost years before he was born."

"Then we should at least tell him so he can make an informed decision. If it could save us time, then we must."

"I'm willing to go either route, though it's not my choice to make."

Isabel got to her feet excitedly and led Bruff off to where Relysis sat and had the miner tell the general about an option that might help them save some time traveling to Pendar. Relysis was definitely interested, though getting specific details from Bruff was difficult and Relysis finally gave the group his thoughts.

"We'll decide as we go. If the option presents itself to go back underground to save some time we can discuss it more then. However, I know the route above ground, having traveled it on many occasions in my lifetime, and that familiarity can't be discounted. That's the general in me talking, and it's a voice I'm loath to ignore."

"That's settled then. We'll get out from under this mountain and see some open skies for a change. My crew is ready when you are, General."

The party took just a bit more time to check their gear and prepare to leave the familiar confines of the city under the mountain. Soon the word was passed around that it was time to move out. Relysis took the lead as they all began to pass through the door. Many of the dwarves from the lost mining crew paused to take in the wonder of all the space they suddenly found themselves in; the glade was small, but the sky above them was endless.

"Come on boys, there are others who need to get out of the mountain. Keep moving along, there will be time to take it all in while we're hiking to Pendar." Bruff tried to keep them from bumping into each other as they stopped and looked skyward.

Isabel sidled over to where Kurad had taken up a station watching over the area, always vigilant in the land of the living and behaving no different in the ghost realm.

"Did you notice how Bruff was less than enthused about taking us through these secret tunnels he told us about?"

"I did. I also noticed that you were not concerned either about going below ground once again. Has your fear of the monsters of the deep receded?"

"Maybe it has." Isabel had to pause as she realized that the weight of the mountain she usually felt had been lifted in the ghost realm. "I think I have just had more on my mind and I didn't have the time to feed my anxiety."

"Wise words."

"Thanks."

"I'm going to scout ahead, would you like to join me? I've heard you are nearly elvish in your abilities."

"Let's go."

Kurad made a quick hand motion to Relysis to let him know their plan before the pair left him with his troop of sightseeing dwarves. Relysis only nodded in response, likely jealous of the pair unencumbered by the miners who were more inclined to mill about than strike out on the trail.

Isabel was thrilled to be invited along with Kurad and she had no intention of letting him down. He was more than just an honorary member of her family, Kurad was legendary in his exploits as a scout. It was why he had been entrusted by her grandfather to save her father from certain death when the gnomes overran the city when Edward was just a boy. She felt there was no one more capable in any situation and anything she could learn directly from him would serve her well in life, and so as they ran through the forest she kept returning her gaze to him.

They had traveled many miles when she turned her eyes towards him once again to see him pause in midstride and crouch low to the ground, for long moments his eyes never leaving the small grouping of trees directly ahead of him. When he finally turned to locate her his hand signals told of the danger they were in and that they needed to go back immediately.

Following his lead she began to backtrack she had come, but she didn't get far before the cries of alarm rang out from all around them. The battle cries from the orcs that came rushing forward through the trees sounding even more terrifying in death than they did when they were amongst the living.

CHAPTER TWENTY SEVEN

"We can't remain on the defensive any longer. Every day we hide behind these walls the dragons' army inches forward."

"How do you propose we do that with dragons flying overhead at all times, day and night? Anytime we try to counterattack, the dragons descend and chase us back with their flames."

"Brother, I need you to get creative. Don't be afraid to step out of my shadow. I'm king here only because that was my title in life."

"You're wrong, but I will promise to look for a strategy that will give us a chance to win some ground back."

"That's all I ask, though if you have something right now I would be willing to listen."

"Just that, come up with a plan to save the kingdom in the next several minutes. I might need to take a nap first."

"Not the entire kingdom, just the castle, oh and to also keep the book safe from the wizard."

Samuel didn't give Stephen a chance to reply, he knew that his request was nearly impossible, but his desperation to throw back the dragons' army was growing with each passing day. Heading out to the ramparts he looked skyward, a habit he loathed that he was forced to adopt, to see where the dragon was at the moment. There was always at least one.

Spotting it at the far end of the city he watched it as it did a lazy circuit around where once upon a time the walls that defended the citizens towered over the landscape. Samuel continued to track the dragon for several more rotations, and with each lap an idea began to form. By the time it finished a handful more, Samuel had a plan he thought might just give his army the victory it sorely needed. If they could gain some ground back it would boost their morale.

Samuel rushed back into the castle, crossing the courtyard littered with large granite blocks, before bounding up the steps and through the remnants of the doorway. Looking about for his brother he ran along the broken corridors, finally finding him alone in the throne room.

"Stephen, I'm glad I found you. I think I have found a way to beat the dragons' army. Actually, you gave me the idea, if only for a night to push them away from the castle."

Stephen looked up at his brother's intrusion, his thoughts elsewhere. "Do you ever wonder about Edward's fate?"

"Sure I do. Every day I walk these halls I wonder how he's doing. I hope he survived the attacks of the dragon on Pendar. We can go ask some of our new archers. They were in the city when reportedly Kurad shot down the dragon. Why do you bring this up now?"

"Edward would be older than both of us now. He could have children who are grown."

"I try to imagine what he's like and if he ever had those children you speak of. Someday we'll gather in the great hall and he can tell us the stories of his life."

"In order to do that we need to beat this dragon. Tell me what I came up with. I'm ready to be done here."

"That's the spirit, I'll tell you on the way." Samuel quickly filled his brother in on his plan as they walked and along the way the pair had gathered their commanders together. It didn't take them long to brief the commanders of the army on what they would need to do and soon there were messengers dispatched to spread the word. The moment to act was now and they didn't want to waste what might be their only opportunity to deal the dragon an unexpected blow.

The plan was being implemented as fast as they could while the scouts placed atop the walls were given strict instructions to track the dragon's flight. Samuel had identified one habit this dragon had during its lazy circuit that would provide them their chance. To his amazement the dragon actually closed its eyes and appeared to nap while it glided away from the castle.

Samuel headed out to take his position at the head of the army as they crowded together at the point of attack inside the courtyard of the castle, his presence alone lifting the spirits of those around him as they all waited anxiously for the signal to come. The tension within the soldiers built with every passing moment as they waited for what they knew was about to happen. Luckily, it didn't take long for a series of low whistles to be passed down from the lookouts above and spread quickly through the ranks.

The gates swung open without any of the usual fanfare of soldiers charging into battle, no rousing cheers to boost their courage as they faced an overwhelming opponent. Instead they streamed out from behind their protective walls and caught their enemy by surprise as they lounged about, confident that the dragon patrolling the skies above would be watching over them, except now it was nearly at the far end of the city and gliding even further out, completely unaware of the silent attack.

Samuel led a large force of dwarves into the opposing army, their battleaxes joining his broadsword in sending many gnomes into the mist as they sliced through their ghostly figures. They didn't slow a step as they pushed the phalanx deeper into the sleeping forces. Samuel had one goal in mind and that was to take back the territory around the castle in a bold rush. There was no time to engage every ghostly gnome they encountered, letting some slip by and get behind him knowing he had archers atop the walls protecting his rear, picking off the enemy with their arrows before they could regroup and counterattack.

The gnomes were scattering before this fresh assault by the dwarves and no matter which way they ran, steel tipped arrows chased them down. Samuel knew they had to be fast in order to clear the area he intended before the dragon heard the cries of his own troops and returned to save them. He was counting down in his head the time remaining before the dragon would arrive and he dared to begin to believe that they were going to get the zone cleared when a pair of trolls lumbered out from the ruins of a nearby building.

"We don't have time to tarry against these two," Samuel growled to the dwarf captain at his elbow and shoved his way forward through a squad of gnomes, his shield before him and sword swinging wildly as the gnomes evaporated before his fury. With a path open before him he raced across the gap to engage the trolls howling in anticipation of meeting the King of Pendar again on the battlefield.

By the time Samuel arrived to do battle with the pair he realized he had outrun his dwarven brethren and was now isolated with the pair of trolls who clearly read the situation in that same moment as he did. Stepping apart from each other they created a lane between them that Samuel had no choice but to enter as he sought to engage them both at the same time without getting crushed by their massive clubs whistling past him. He dove to the ground and rolled away as he sliced at the nearest troll's thick legs.

He knew he had struck a solid blow as the sword nearly slipped from his hand and the troll's howl turned to pain. Skidding to a stop he jumped to his feet, but was immediately forced to jump to his side as another club barely missed his head. A blow that would have surely sent him into the mist and left his army without their king this day. There was no time to dwell on that as the other troll moved to intercept his avenue of escape.

The blow Samuel delivered to the troll's leg saved him as it was just a split second too slow to catch up to him as he skittered beyond their reach. Unfortunately, they seemed to have fought side by side in the past and knew what they needed to do without speaking a word to each other. They had Samuel on the run again before he could launch any type of attack against them.

Desperation forced him to keep on the move as he maneuvered around the small arena the combatants had created around them. With every moment that passed he knew even without looking skyward the dragon was surely on its way. He even thought he heard its rage above the trolls' howling, but he couldn't be sure. Regardless he was all too aware that the battle was turning against him and, unless something changed, the fight would be lost along with the battle to take back ground from the wizard.

In that next moment the help he needed arrived in the form of a wall of shields held by a squad of charging dwarves who didn't pause for even a heartbeat before they slammed into the trolls from behind. The trolls and dwarves went down in a heap when the dwarves took their legs out from under them and kept churning forward. Once on the ground the dwarves had the advantage and soon dispatched the trolls into the mist.

Samuel rushed over to give his rescuers a hand to their feet, but their celebration was interrupted by an ear piercing scream from above as the dragon swooped low over the battlefield, its fire washing away any ghost soldiers left out in the open. The dwarves with Samuel did their best to create a barrier above them with their shields, but many were wisped away with the dragon fire.

Gripping his own shield as the flames licked at his arm he gritted his teeth and hung onto the only thing that could save him from the terrible fire. Then, as suddenly as the dragon had descended, it was past them and climbing high into the sky. Samuel pulled down his shield to watch its ascent. He knew he didn't have time to help his few remaining soldiers get to safety so he reached down and tightened the strap that held his shield to his arm and called those scattered about to rally to him so that together they could win the day.

There were only a handful of them crouching beneath their shields when the dragon passed overhead again. The intense heat beneath the shields was nearly unbearable as the dragon let loose with his flames once more. Just as the fire came to an end the ground beneath their feet shook, causing Samuel and the dwarves to dance about to keep upright. Dropping his shield, Samuel knew exactly what would be facing him as the smoke began to clear.

"Get out of here boys. He's here for me, now run." Samuel left no room for the handful of dwarves to do anything else but obey their king and he was soon standing in front of the majestic beast alone.

"You think to save them, do you?" The air reverberated as the dragon spoke to Samuel.

"It's a gesture you never figured out in life, and you are no smarter in death."

"I'm not even going to argue with you. That's not why I'm here. We both know what I want. I just need to know what you are willing to sacrifice to keep it from me."

"I can't think of anything that will change my mind after all this time."

"Don't be so sure of your resolve, I haven't even begun to test you yet. I will give you this victory tonight, but know that it is a gift that I can take back at anytime, and know that I will. Next time I will bring my son and we will finish this. It's a shame you won't have that same support."

Dungarvan laughed as he launched himself into the air, sending a giant ball of flame into the sky to punctuate his promise as Samuel stood and watched from below. He wasn't sure what the wizard meant by his statement, but it wasn't hard for Samuel to imagine what the dragon meant to put his army through in his attempt to wrest the book from Samuel's hands. What Dungarvan didn't know was his resolve to protect his own blood in the realm of the living where he believed his own son still reigned.

CHAPTER TWENTY EIGHT

"Why does Dungarvan drag this out? He brought us all here for a reason."

"He has decided he needs to wait for the upcoming solstice, when the night is the longest. It will add energy to his spells, according to him."

"How long away is that? I'm getting bored sitting in this hollowed out building."

"I'm not sure you should be looking forward to this event."

"It's an event now?"

"There was always going to be some pageantry to Dungarvan forcing your grandfather to trade the book for his grandson's life."

"What did you say?"

"Probably too much, but I'm bored too. If Orgle knew I was back in Pendar he would likely come looking for me to extract some punishment for his failures, so I'm stuck here watching over you."

"I could care less about you and Orgle. You said my grandfather is here?"

"Of course he is, who else would be bothering to try and protect what is left of the city?"

"Well, it could be any number of kings, or even generals, who have died defending these walls that lead the army against Dungarvan's forces."

"Dungarvan probably wishes it was anyone else, well not anyone. Luckily that won't be a problem."

"Quit talking to him." Rathlin came into the room where Samuel was being held and barked the command at the gnome.

Kropett slunk away leaving Samuel wishing he had finished his conversation with the little gnome. He had learned some important facts, yet he felt he was on the verge of learning much more. He decided to focus on what he had learned. His grandfather, the man he was named after, was leading the force opposing the wizards and that alone gave him something to cling to.

Samuel wasn't sure how he could use the information about his grandfather yet, but Kropett had also mentioned a book that Dungarvan apparently coveted greatly. The wizard had gone to great lengths to bring Samuel to this ghostly realm in order to trade him with his grandfather. He paused in his thinking, mulling that fact over in his mind. Dungarvan had been dead as long as Samuel had been alive, they actually shared that very date. What else linked the pair? Was is just that twist of fate when Dungarvan failed to kill Samuel as a newborn and was slain himself that the wizard still obsessed over?

Samuel realized then what Kropett had meant when he said that he wasn't going to enjoy the upcoming event. This wasn't just going to be a trade for the book the gnome had mentioned, no this was all being put together to finish what Dungarvan had failed to do those many years ago on the Galway bridge over the Ballaghaderreen Falls. Kropett had said too much and revealed the truth of what was going to happen. Samuel needed to find a way to stop the ceremony.

Rathlin stayed with the pair the rest of that night, leaving only when Dungarvan came back from wherever he spent his time, landing heavily before he shed his dragon disguise. Samuel had noted that the pair spent little time together and that they took turns shifting into their dragon personas before launching into the sky on a constant rotation. There were sounds of battle that reached his ears from time to time so he imagined that their only purpose to fly about as dragons was to harass his grandfather's army and those who fought beside him.

With Kropett revealing at least a part of the elaborate plot for Dungarvan to exact his revenge, Samuel's mind turned to figuring out how to get out of his current predicament and thwart the wizard one more time. The opportunities would be few based on the past several days and there were far too few moments where he was left alone with the little gnome. Given the escalation in battle sounds he assumed he only had a few days to come up with a plan and act on it.

He spent the rest of that day waiting patiently for any opportunity for him to be alone with the gnome. At the moment he felt Kropett was the closest chance of creating an ally, or at least an unwitting one. He had already told him too much, why would he not tell him more given the chance? The wizards treated him little better than they did their prisoner, the only tangible difference were the bindings that kept Samuel tied to the support post in the building they used for their base.

It was as the day was growing darker that Kropett came running into the room and roused Dungarvan speaking excitedly, his words coming out in a jumble. The wizard was annoyed, but got to his feet, pushing Kropett out of his way as he was leaving the room to see to whatever had the little gnome worked up. Samuel saw his chance and called softly to the gnome sprawled out on the floor across the way from him.

"Kropett, are you okay? Dungarvan had no right to push you down like that."

"He's just tired of waiting," Kropett said as he got back to his feet.

"No, he is always mean to you. I see it all the time and it's not right to treat you like that. You should tell him to stop, or I could for you."

"It's only for a little while longer. Once we get the book and Dungarvan transforms us all we can go back to the land of the living, and then I'm going to get as far away from them as I can."

Samuel could hear lots of shouting from outside the building and it had Kropett visibly cringing as he looked about for a place to hide.

"Come over here behind my post. Whoever is out there won't see you if they come in."

"It's Orgle, he is impatient for the event too."

"Did Dungarvan agree to bring him back to the living with us too?"

"There will only be a few going, Dungarvan, Rathlin, and hopefully myself if I play along with them for a couple more days."

Samuel's heart sank at Kropett's statement. There was no way the little gnome was going to betray his master if it was his only chance to leave the ghost realm behind and return to his life. He needed to abandon his idea of using him as his accomplice in getting free. If it was going to happen it would have to be accomplished on his own.

In frustration, he tugged once again at his restraints as he had countless times before. However, this time he felt overwhelmed by the futility of his situation and didn't care if the little gnome saw him or not.

"Hey, knock it off. You're not getting free of those before Dungarvan allows you to."

"Oh, is he going to kill me more than once? It seems a hollow threat if that is already the plan."

"No, but he can make it a lot worse on you before and after."

"I don't follow. What can be worse than existing here forever? You seem to be doing okay other than dreaming about whatever pathetic life you left behind."

"He'll vanquish your spirit from even this realm. You will be lost forever as if you were reduced to a mist that could never reform."

"Is that part of his spell then? He's going to threaten my grandfather to send me there?"

"Not exactly." Kropett's eyes darted to Samuel's sword lying on the table across the room and away again so quickly that Samuel wasn't sure if he had imagined it or not.

There was no more time to talk as Dungarvan came back into the room after breaking off his heated discussion with Orgle. Kropett slid casually away from where he had been standing during his discussion with Samuel, clearly hoping the wizard had not taken undue notice of the happenings.

"Kropett, what have I told you? You two have nothing to talk about with one another. If I catch you uttering even one word to the prisoner I'm going to hand you over to Orgle to be his play thing for the rest of eternity."

Samuel wasn't sure if he believed his ears, but he was almost sure that he heard the little gnome yelp before he took several strides to put as much distance between them as possible without even so much as a backward glance. He knew that Dungarvan's threat would bring any help he sought from the little gnome to an end. He leaned back against the post, determined he was up to the task of escaping from the wizard.

He wasn't sure how, but he knew he needed to get back home and let his family know he was okay. There had been no opportunity to let them know where he was other than his brief call for help to Kurad. He hoped his protector would find the ring he left him as proof, and somehow come to his rescue. It had been so long ago he felt he was at the point that he could not afford to hang onto that hope any longer, even if he wanted to still believe. In the end he whispered into the darkness.

"Kurad, if you can hear me I hope you know where I am and can come soon."

The Ghosts of Pendar

CHAPTER TWENTY NINE

The sounds of battle came from just ahead, he quickened his pace even more. He had been tracking their party for several days and just as he closed in, they had become embroiled in a conflict. Muted shouts drifting through the haze were familiar to his ears and he raced forward, pulling his battleaxe free from where it hung at his back.

Racing past dwarves engaged with orc warriors he sought to reach the one voice that came clear to him, his daughter, Isabel. Broad strokes of his axe cleared away every orc who tried to intercept him and keep him from coming to Isabel's aid. He could see from afar she was pressed hard to keep a handful of orcs at the end of her blade.

Orcs scattered before him as they witnessed the savage fury of the man with the giant battleaxe tearing through their ranks. The last to turn tail and run were those engaged with the princess. They too finally ran off as he arrived, allowing him to stop just behind her.

"Kurad, have you ever seen such a thing. Where did they all go?" Isabel asked as she turned to look for Kurad who had been fighting off to the side. It was then she saw the man standing behind her. "Father! What are you doing here?"

"I saw that you needed some help."

"Yes, thank you. Kurad and I came upon this pack of orcs when we were scouting for our party. What happened to you? You were supposed to stay behind and watch over our bodies. We had to send the mayor back. Did you see him?"

"I crossed paths with the mayor and he made it back to his body just as you planned. I agree that it wasn't the plan for me to come, but some decisions aren't left up to us. Right, Kurad." Edward looked to his friend and protector of the crown. Edward could tell by the look in his eyes he knew the truth. The bond between them would have signaled his death as clear as a single bell on a still night.

"You have to make the most of what fate delivers to you. It is good to see you, though I wish the circumstances were different."

Edward held back his urge to embrace the man who had been such a big part of his life. His desire to shield Isabel from the truth for the time being kept him as arms length, instead clasping forearms as was the custom. Holding their grip for a moment longer, Edward fought to keep his emotions in check before he released him and turned to Isabel.

"Now how about a hug from my daughter? I know I wasn't supposed to be here, but I did rescue you."

"Of course, though you're not off the hook. We're going to discuss this later." Isabel moved close and allowed herself to be enveloped into her father's arms.

Edward fought back tears as he held her diminutive childlike form tight. A flood of memories from her childhood cascaded through his mind, and too the knowledge that there was precious little time to create more before they parted ways until they met again at the end of her lifetime.

Kurad came to his rescue, calling everyone to gather around and introducing Edward to the party traveling together to Pendar. "This is King Edward Ellingstone, father of our Isabel and Samuel who we intend to rescue from the wizard. Please make him feel welcome, he's new here."

"I'm Bruff, I've been the leader of this mining outfit for the last thousand years or so. I thought when we left the mine behind that we could help win your boy's freedom, however, with the way you swing that magnificent battleaxe I think I will just stay behind you and take care of any you might miss. Tralee told us there is some dwarf blood in your veins, I won't dispute that none."

"It's my pleasure to meet you all and I will not turn away any help that is offered."

"I do have one question for you, what master craftsman created that battleaxe of yours? Say it surely was a dwarf, or may my beard fall off."

"Careful now lest you lose that fine beard. He is actually a human, though he studied under the best dwarven smithies in all of Dulin. He still walks among the living so you'll have to wait a spell before he arrives to take orders here."

"Things have certainly changed in the last several centuries," Bruff said as he tugged nervously at his beard, seemingly afraid that it may indeed fall off for his lost wager.

"I think we need to be moving along, I'm sure I heard a whisper on the wind that Samuel is in need of our help."

"You heard him again?" Isabel was quick to jump on Kurad's intimation.

"It seemed to come from a distance, which would make me believe they are in Pendar now."

"Isabel, are you and Kurad ready to pick up where you left off and lead us the rest of the way to Pendar?"

"That depends on if Bruff is ready to show us the underground tunnels they used so many centuries ago. With the orcs roaming the mountainsides and the urgency of Samuel's message, it might be time to change our path. At this point, it might be the fastest route."

"Is she right, Bruff? You know of a quicker way to get to Pendar without dealing with anymore orcs."

"When I spoke of them before I immediately regretted making mention of them. I refrained from stating it outright before, but there are things down in the tunnels that would make you think that running into a few orcs might be a better option, and truth be told there are a few in my crew who are here because of them."

"Let's stay above ground then. I think we can all agree that we don't need to be waking up any beasts from the underworld. We can leave that exploration for another adventure." Edward watched the tension gathered in Isabel's body upon Bruff's admission release at his decision. He knew she still carried fears of the dagar with her and was even a little surprised that she had been advocating taking the underground tunnels.

"We better get moving before these orcs regroup and overcome their fear of the axe wielding ghost king to come back for more." Kurad motioned for Isabel to accompany him and they were quick to strike out ahead of the party.

"Don't get far ahead of us, I don't want to have to come to your rescue again." Per his command they didn't range out too far ahead of the group Edward has assumed command of, the distance giving him the opportunity to talk to his trusted general. Relysis had been unusually quiet since his arrival, a fact which changed immediately once Edward fell in next to him on the trail.

"You're a fool, boy, if you don't think she'll figure it out soon enough. If I wasn't angry enough at you for whatever happened to bring you here, that would do it too."

"Whenever she finds out it will be too soon. I don't want her to be distracted. How did you know?"

"You're as good with that axe of yours now as you were when you were half your age. It's a good thing she had her back to you when you were cutting your way through their ranks or she would have known straight away too. What happened?"

"My age and my injuries as you would point out. He slipped in behind me after you three departed. Caught me without my blade, not that it would have made a difference. He was as much alive as I was at the time. He wore an amulet around his neck." Edward pulled the dragon's claw clutching a blue stone from his jacket pocket to show the general.

"How did you come to have this?"

"I tracked him down in whatever realm this is, and with my youth restored and injuries no longer hindering me, I exacted a bit of revenge. My guess is he won't get back to the living without this trinket, one I assume came from the wizard."

"It's a good bet that you're right. Dungarvan has been behind this plot from the beginning, so there's no reason to believe he wouldn't send someone to make sure there wasn't anyone coming to Samuel's rescue."

"The less he knows about us coming, the better our chances are of surprising him."

"Then we better get there fast, it seems he's already there and we've no idea what he's got planned with his army."

Edward paused for a moment as his mind drifted ahead to the city the dragon destroyed. Why did Dungarvan pick Pendar? His castle had been far away in Sligo, there must be something else there that drew him to that location. What was he after and why would he have an army positioned there to help him? It was then that the possibility struck him.

"If there is an army defending Pendar from Dungarvan, who would be leading it?"

"I see where you're going with this. All I'm going to say is that I'm still mad at you, but a reunion of that sort might take the edge off my mood just a bit."

"Me too." Edward slapped Relysis on the back as his emotions surged. "Let's hope."

The Ghosts of Pendar

CHAPTER THIRTY

"There are reports from the wall that the wizard's army is amassing just outside our perimeter to the north."

"He told me he would take it back from me, but he is going to have to earn it," Samuel declared, looking up at his brother from where he was seated in the old dining hall.

"Those messages also state that Orgle has been sighted along with a handful of trolls within the force."

"Any word of wizards or dragons lurking beyond our wall?"

"Neither have been sighted yet."

"So the question is whether this is his final battle to gain the book he seeks."

"With the numbers he has gathered it would seem so."

"I'm not convinced. Dungarvan wouldn't trust Orgle to get this right. Stay alert to this being a big show of strength beyond our walls so that he can distract us."

"Where are you going?"

"It seems Orgle has requested my presence, you said as much just now."

Samuel grabbed his gear, always close at hand, off the table and headed for the wall. He knew that Dungarvan would try to overrun their defenses at some point, and if he could do it without his dragon fire, even the better. It could explain why there wasn't a dragon lurking about ready to assist the battle.

His son though, would love nothing more than to destroy the city once again and claim victory a second time. That was reason enough to believe this wasn't going to be the final battle, but if it wasn't what was the wizard waiting for? Samuel walked through the remnants of his castle, passing soldiers running to their battle stations as he pondered the question.

He was no closer to the answer when he stepped outside and witnessed the army that had assembled across from his own. The sheer size of it struck him then and made him realize that the dragons might not be needed. His eyes were drawn far and wide to the wizard's army stretching beyond the expanse of the north wall of the castle and disappearing into the distance only when they overflowed the avenues leading up to the castle.

Bringing his gaze back to the leading edge of the army he immediately focused on the squad of trolls at the forefront, their numbers greater than he remembered seeing at any one time in all his time in the ghost realm. Beyond that there were gnomes uncountable led by no other than the largest and cruelest of them all, Orgle who was whipping them up into a frenzy with his antics as he stood atop a mound of a collapsed building and extorted them into a bloodlust fever.

Samuel's troops by comparison were sedate. They had battled these gnomes more times than any of them they would care to count. Instead a nervous energy coursed through them, unintentionally feeding the same emotion to those around them. Samuel had seen it too many times where the battle was lost even before it began when the troops collectively lost their nerve and will to fight. He sensed that now and knew he had to do something to get them engaged and ready to repel the force that threatened.

He picked up his pace as he moved along the parapet, weaving his way around blocks of granite that littered his path, jumping over cracks that crisscrossed the wall. Finally arriving at the point across the wall from Orgle he leapt up to the top of the tallest outcropping he could find, pausing for a moment to survey the mass of warriors on both sides of the battle line that had formed.

Standing silently he waited for his own soldiers to take notice, their voices growing silent as word spread of the king's presence. It wasn't long for Orgle to see him too. The rivalry the two shared for all these long years got the better of him and he let his focus shift from his own warriors to Samuel.

Samuel hid his smile from the big gnome. He had hoped, even anticipated Orgle's reaction, and meant to use it to his advantage as the gnomes assembled across from his dwarves fell silent. Standing tall he looked from one end to the other, nodding approvingly to his soldiers as they began to feed off his energy. He knew he commanded the crowd now and began theatrics of his own, though his style was completely opposite of Orgle's.

"So you are going to throw your soldiers onto my dwarves' axes again today." His statement directed at the gnome leader drew a shout of approval from the dwarves staged below him. "How about we save you the effort and you just go back to your beds and get a good night's rest? It would be better than expiring into the mist."

His own soldiers were the ones getting their boost now. Their battle chants started with a few individuals here and there before spreading beyond the scattered pockets until his whole army had taken them up. On the other side of the wall the gnomes, even with their superior numbers, began to shrink back from the thunderous voices that rose into the still air.

Samuel let it build for a while before he held up his hand asking for their silence. It took a while longer for them to cease their chants than it did to get them going, but eventually it tapered off and they all looked up to him expectantly. He knew what they needed and he gave it to them. Reaching back, he drew his giant broadsword from where it hung at his back and pulled it free, swinging it in an exaggerated arc, only stopping when he held it straight overhead to punctuate the statement that came next.

"Who's ready to send some gnomes into the mist today?" He didn't wait for the cheering to stop before he took a step back and then rushed forward, launching himself off the wall and down into the mass of dwarves that waited below to catch him.

While the gnomes were enraptured with the king's leap, the archers stationed along the wall let loose with several volleys of arrows that shredded the front lines of the Orgle's army and sent them into the mist. Without stopping, they continued their assault from above and cleared a path for Samuel and the dwarves to throw open the gates and rush out into the void they created.

With the element of surprise Samuel and the dwarves were able to drive deep into the front ranks of the gnomes. As the dwarves engaged the enemy, every swing of an axe cut into the gnomes' numbers and they were diminishing rapidly, allowing more dwarves to funnel out onto the battlefield to join in. Samuel kept pushing deeper into Orgle's army with his forces right behind him.

He knew this momentum wouldn't continue, but he wanted to punish Orgle as much as he could before the weight of the opposing army shifted the scales. The rout by his forces continued for longer than even he had anticipated and only ended when Orgle's trolls rumbled into the fray. With the new combatants joining the battle the gnome army suddenly stiffened their resolve as the trolls, stepping forward in lockstep, created a barrier as impenetrable as any granite wall the dwarves could have built. Samuel, however, had more confidence in their shields.

"Boys," Samuel's voice called out over the tumult surrounding his soldiers. "Form up a shield wall, the trolls have come to save the gnomes again."

Dwarves immediately began to disengage with the gnomes they were fighting and dropped back to give their king the wall of shields he called for. Samuel knew the odds of turning back the hulking beasts across from them were slim, but he didn't give the dwarves lining up with him a moment to hesitate. Looking about he waited for the last of them to lock his shield to the dwarf next to him before he gave the order.

"Advance!" With the simple order the first rank of dwarves stepped out with their shields facing the trolls. The rows in reserve moved forward at the same pace holding their shields aloft to protect those at the front. At the middle of the shield wall was Samuel and his dwarven wrought shield, the crest of the King of Pendar visible to all lined across from them, marching forward along with his dwarven brothers.

As the dwarves, with Samuel at the forefront, inched forward the trolls howled in anticipation. Orgle stood behind them screaming at them to rush into the dwarven wall, but they moved at their own pace. Samuel had seen this too many times, he knew the trolls would eventually heed their leader and begin their charge. Everyone in the shield wall knew it too, they didn't need to be told. Samuel spoke the words regardless.

"Steady, they are going to charge any moment now. Protect the dwarf to either side of you, keep your shields locked. Make them pay dearly for any breach they may try to make."

Looking up Samuel could see arrows from his men stationed on the walls streaking overhead as they harassed the trolls, not allowing them to focus on the dwarves who continued to creep forward. Gnomes sprinted out across the divide to try and do the same to the dwarves and stop their advance. Each was met with the same fate as a small fissure would open in the wall and a dwarf with a battleaxe would slip out and send the gnome into the mist before stepping back and sealing the wall behind them.

Samuel let the dwarves enjoy their little victories for now, it kept them engaged, and not focused on the overwhelming challenge the trolls presented. He knew at any moment the trolls would build up the courage to charge their shields. Hanging onto that thought he moved the line forward. As daunting as the trolls were across from him, the dwarves weren't to be taken lightly either.

Many armies had charged into battle against the dwarves and had their armies break when they collided with the strength of the warriors behind the dwarven steel. The trolls were aware of this too and Samuel took a small amount of pleasure in the respect his boys had earned. However, he also knew the trolls would be overcoming that respect point very soon. It was almost as if Orgle read his mind when the big gnome screamed out his order to charge.

The trolls and their ponderous gait were slow to get moving, the gnomes off to either side quickly outgained them and rushed toward the dwarves' defense. There were no openings now as the dwarves gritted their teeth, shouted encouragement to each other, and clung tightly to their shields.

The gnome force crashed into the wall. Their shields held strong as the dwarves dug in their feet and absorbed the weight of the collision. Gnomes kept coming even as those in front smashed into the wall and couldn't go further. The ones coming behind trampled those who tried and failed to breach the defenses of the dwarves. Portions of their line began to bend even as dwarves from behind pushed forward to add to their collective strength.

It was then, when the dwarves had been pushed to their limit to throw the gnome attack back, that the trolls ran headlong into the middle of the line where Samuel himself stood tall. The king, just like his dwarven brothers, held his position as long as he could but then the wall broke and he was shoved backwards, riding the momentum of the trolls as they decimated the shield wall.

Landing hard on his back Samuel lost his shield, torn away by the club of the troll that suddenly loomed over him. Howling in glee the troll stomped on Samuel's sword so he couldn't lift it in his defense as he lined up for the swing that would send the king into the mist and allow Orgle's army to overwhelm the dwarves.

The Ghosts of Pendar

CHAPTER THIRTY ONE

"There is a lot of noise coming from the far side of the city, or rather what is left of it." Isabel observed, squatting down low in the trees to keep from being seen by any lookouts.

"That has to be by the castle. Kurad, where did you encounter the ghosts when you were here?" Edward looked to his friend.

"They were more active the closer I got to the castle, as if I was getting too close to their territory."

"Then we need to get there, and fast."

"Have Relysis bring up the dwarves, we all need to be ready to move quickly."

Kurad disappeared into the trees to give Relysis the order to bring the squad of miners up to where Isabel and Edward waited.

"You said we need to be quick about getting in there. Do you have an idea how to do that?"

"You're the king, or were the king. I was expecting maybe you had a secret way to get in and out of there that you might not have told me about."

"I wish that were the case, but no. The walls were always supposed to be the defense and as long as we were on the inside then we would be safe."

"I hadn't seen the destruction yet. I'm not sure I would be able to come back here in the realm of the living."

"Someday you will."

"How about you?"

"I don't believe my body is made for traveling anymore. You and Samuel can make those decisions when you return."

"You seem invigorated in this world. Almost as if you're young again. Maybe you can figure out how to take this renewed youth back with you."

"Unfortunately that's one thing I'm sure isn't a possibility. How about we just enjoy it while we're both still here?"

Kurad arrived with the balance of their party effectively bringing the pair's conversation to an end. Edward couldn't have been more pleased with the timing, he was beginning to think that his daughter too had guessed the truth of his being there.

"What did you two come up with?"

"Actually I was waiting for the general to suggest something, but maybe you're more adept at getting in and out of places secretly than he is."

"I will not comment on that, however, I feel we need to get to the portion of the wall that is closest to the castle and make our way up and over whatever remains. It will give us our shortest route once inside the walls."

"It's what I would have recommended too," Relysis spoke upon his approach. "Whatever is going on at the castle will likely leave the rest of the city unguarded."

"Then it is settled. Kurad lead the way, Isabel and I will follow and Relysis you bring the dwarves forward when we give you the signal."

Relysis did nothing more than grunt in response. Edward felt bad relegating the general to a glorified babysitter, but until they had a clear path forward they needed to be kept out of sight. A force their size would be noticed if they were out in the open for too long and a response would likely be sent.

Kurad barely waited for Edward to finish speaking before he was off and running. Isabel was right behind him and Edward was suddenly in danger of being left behind with the disgruntled Relysis and his charges. Taking off, he pushed hard and caught his daughter before they reached the edge of the forest. Kurad was already working his way across the field.

Edward looked ahead in the direction Kurad was heading and could easily tell where his mentor had chosen to go over the wall. Tapping Isabel on the shoulder, he sent her running in a crouch just as Kurad had, while sticking to his trail. Edward continued to watch until Kurad reached the wall before he followed suit as Isabel had.

By the time Isabel reached the wall Kurad had already begun clambering up the rubble that had been the city's defense for generations. She followed without hesitation. Edward reached the base of the wall in time to see Isabel slip between a pair of granite blocks and disappear into the haze. Edward gave one last look back to see that Relysis and the miners had reached the edge of the forest. Waiting for a moment to make sure the general had located him, he began his climb.

Pulling himself upward he realized how truly amazing his daughter was. In places, the reach was nearly beyond his outstretched fingers and yet Isabel had scaled the wall without a moment's hesitation. Spurred on to try and match her agility he quickly realized after a couple slips that there was no way for him to be her equal and settled on a more cautious approach.

Looking about when he finally reached the top it took him a few moments to locate the pair crouching low behind a granite block down on the street level. He watched for several moments to make sure there wasn't a threat to them before he began his descent. While he scoured the landscape for any dangers Isabel turned back to him signaling to him that it was all clear.

Arriving at the bottom of the wall, Edward joined Kurad and Isabel before the three spread out and set up a perimeter while the dwarves with Relysis made their way over the wall. It seemed like an eternity for Edward as they could all hear the sounds of battle getting louder. The gnomes' chanting made the air vibrate as it echoed through the deserted city.

By the time Relysis had his crew staged behind them the chorus of gnomes had gone deathly quiet. Edward wasn't sure if that was better or worse, his instincts told him that whatever was happening was coming to a boiling point. Kurad sensed it too and was looking expectantly at him to see if they were ready to move forward. Relysis nodded when Edward signaled him and, with that, they were once again on the run.

Their group quickly spread into a long line as they coursed through the debris littered streets. Kurad, at the lead, continually searched for a clear path that avoided any of the wizards' patrols that may also be out on the same streets. The longer they ran the more evident it became the entire army had been called together, leaving no one to give the alarm.

They knew the city like the back of their hands, even in its current state, and that knowledge gave them an edge as they plotted their course. It wasn't until Edward nearly ran into Kurad and Isabel who had stopped just around a corner when they realized how large the enemy's army was. Ahead of them were the gnomes staged at the back of the charge, held in reserve until their numbers could be brought to bear.

Easing backwards the three of them slipped back around the corner, stopping to hear if they had been noticed. It was then they could hear a voice call out in the common tongue, though they couldn't make out what was said through the chorus of dwarf chants filling the air.

"We need to hurry," Kurad said as he turned to Edward. "That voice was familiar to me, and likely you too."

Edward paused for a moment as he remembered that voice from so many years ago when he was just a young boy. The emotions flooding back to him nearly made his legs weak, threatening to wash him away as he considered the reunion he had dreamt about so many times. It was only Isabel's voice that cut through and brought him back to the present.

"Father, we have to go. Kurad says the battle is eminent."

Edward shook his head as he realized that he must have missed Kurad's words. "We have to get around these gnomes. Follow me."

Taking the lead, he set out on a path he prayed was open to them so they could circumvent the army blocking their way. It was a long shot, but after all this time he knew nothing else other than to get to his father's side. Running without concern for whether the rest of his companions were pacing him or not he dodged down alleys, leaping over blocks that threatened to bar his path forward.

They were still a short distance away when the sounds of battle replaced the chorus of chants. The two sides having reached a fevered pitch were now engaged in a struggle to see which army would win the day. Edward knew the gnome army was large with how far it stretched away from the castle and couldn't imagine the ghosts of Pendar had a fraction of those numbers so he ran on, not stopping until he collided with the backs of a squad of gnomes already pushing forward to join the fight.

Coming on to them too abruptly to stop himself, he reached for his battleaxe and began clearing a path forward as many gnomes evaporated into the mist about him. Soon Kurad and Isabel joined in with Relysis bringing the miners forward into the fray. With the extra blades at his side they increased their speed, decimating the gnomes who had not yet recognized they were being attacked from behind. The rout continued for several long minutes until the gnomes realized what was happening to their companions and they turned to fight.

Edward's attack stalled, forcing him to call for help as they suddenly faced stiffer resistance. His cry was rewarded with a streaking Kurad, his sword slashing a path to him. Isabel and Relysis were soon at his side as well, and together they began moving forward once again with the miners adding their weapons to their flanks.

The Ghosts of Pendar

Before long the band had reached the grounds outside the castle and could see firsthand the battle raging between the two forces. The gnomes threw themselves against the shield wall while a squad of trolls were wading forward, crushing any gnomes who didn't get clear of them before they reached the dwarven defense. The trolls had begun to break through. It was as the shield wall fell apart that he first laid eyes on who he knew instantly was his father, but he was knocked backwards and disappeared within the chaos.

Edward immediately rushed forward towards the troll bearing down on where he knew his father must be. Gnomes who tried to stop his progress were no match for his fury and he closed the gap, emerging through the haze to see his father prone before the troll, his club aimed directly at the man. Without even thinking he kept up his momentum and bowled over anyone who tried to stop him. His eyes were focused on one thing only.

Waiting until the last moment, he finally shouted out a warning to the troll to distract its swing. The brief hesitation was all he needed to close the distance, his magnificent axe slicing clean through the extended arm of the troll. The shocked troll stopped and stared in disbelief at his arm lying on the ground before him, giving Edward the opportunity he needed to catch it with his backswing and sent it into the mist.

Edward turned to the man lying on the ground looking up at him in disbelief just as the troll had. Reaching down to grab his hand he finally spoke.

"Father, we need to get out of here."

CHAPTER THIRTY TWO

"Why aren't we out there?" Rathlin screamed at his father, "We could finish this battle tonight and the book is ours."

"This is just a skirmish. Orgle was voicing his frustration so I gave him the go ahead to see what he could do if we pulled in all our forces."

"Except the dragons."

"Yes, except the dragons." Dungarvan nodded his head to Rathlin.

Samuel listened to the exchange from his position across the room tied to the post. He was surprised Dungarvan was allowing the young upstart wizard to berate him without any reprisal. The two seemed to be ignoring him so he kept his head down and continued to act disinterested.

"Then what are we waiting for? We have the boy king and his sword, what else is there?"

"The solstice is almost here."

"Why are we waiting until this solstice event, why not just help Orgle tonight and finish this once and for all?"

"Even if we sent all of the king's army into the mist with our dragon fire they would all be returned before we can utilize the book. Then there will be nothing but distractions while we try to perform the ceremony."

"Do it tonight instead. Orgle, with his advantage in numbers, surely has Samuel's army on the brink of destruction."

"It needs to be on the longest night. The pathway is the shortest between the worlds of the living and dead."

Samuel tried not to react to the Rathlin's claim that Orgle's army would be able to defeat the ghosts of Pendar led by his grandfather. He had not seen anything of either side's forces since being brought here and had no idea the size of each army.

He didn't know what the plan was, but he was sure he didn't want to be a part of it. Unfortunately he had yet to figure out a way to escape his keepers and time was running out. Out of habit he tugged on the bindings again with the same result as the hundreds of times he had done so before.

"Kropett, make sure the boy is secured."

Samuel's activity had not gone unnoticed by Dungarvan and the gnome was quick to scurry over to make sure he was still bound adequately. It was hard for Samuel to hear what the wizards were saying as the gnome rustled about so he leaned around him.

"Why don't you just let me send him into the mist with a bit of dragon fire so we don't have to watch over him?"

"Don't be a fool," Dungarvan snapped at his son. "He is not in this realm like the rest of us. If he dies here that is the end of all of these years of planning. With his death in this realm he will be lost to the world of the living and will do me no good. I need that tether he and the sword provide to pull myself back to the living."

There was a long pause between the two while Samuel waited for the volatile Rathlin to respond to his father's reprimand. Instead, the young wizard appeared to let the matter lie, and in place of responding, he stalked out of the room. Samuel was unsure if the young wizard had not heard his father's plan as Samuel had. He was sure if he had there would have been an explosive reaction. Dungarvan had clearly stated this was all for his benefit alone. Possibly the older wizard misspoke but he doubted it. He knew enough of Dungarvan's reputation to believe the wizard meant exactly what he said.

Looking over at Kropett Samuel sensed by the crafty little gnome's body language there was a distinct possibility that he too had heard Dungarvan's true intentions. Samuel could only hope he had, it would be his best chance yet to convince the gnome that he should help him escape to repay the wizard's duplicity. If only he could get some time alone with Kropett to convince him it was a good idea to sever ties with the wizard.

The night dragged on, the sounds of battle ebbing and flowing throughout as armies squared off one more time in advance of the event Dungarvan had planned. Samuel couldn't help but wonder if either side knew that this war, the one that had been playing out over the ages, was nearly over. The wizards' army had all been manipulated by Dungarvan and none of them would know the truth until the wizard escaped death's clutches and returned to the world of the living without them.

After a long night alone with his thoughts Samuel determined his only hope remained in somehow convincing Kropett to carry word to Orgle and his army that Dungarvan was going to double cross them. The only problem with his plan was that the wizard remained in the room with them through the night. Samuel couldn't talk to the gnome like he desperately needed to and he didn't see that changing so he gave into the need to rest, his eyes shutting out the haze as he let sleep take him away for at least a little while.

Coming awake with a start, yanking on his bindings, he sought to put his hands up before him as he stared directly into Kropett's eyes. The gnome sat mere inches away from him.

"What are you doing?"

"Quiet, you'll alert the wizard."

"You heard what he said, didn't you? He's going to leave you here with Orgle," Samuel whispered under his breath, eyes scanning their surroundings to find the wizard.

"Yes."

"And you're okay with that? You've been serving him for more years than I can imagine and now he plans on just discarding you."

"No, though I had considered the possibility more than once. He says things around me as if I'm not here that he shouldn't, but I thought he would change his mind."

"Release me, I can't promise that I can return you to the living, but I will do everything I can to not let Dungarvan return either."

"He would torture me forever."

Samuel wasn't sure what to say, the little gnome wasn't wrong. If Dungarvan's plan failed as a result of Kropett releasing him there would be no end to his suffering. Samuel never got the chance. The wizard's voice boomed out from the doorway.

"NEVER TALK TO HIM! I have told you too many times and yet you continue your whisperings," Dungarvan spat the words, pulling his sword free from his scabbard. "It's time I taught you a lesson you would do well to learn."

Raising his blade over the cowering gnome he made a quick downward slash that sent Kropett into the mist in a blink of an eye. Samuel watched in disbelief as the gnome evaporated and left him staring up at the wizard. He wasn't sure where the words came from, but he mustered up his courage in face of the enraged wizard.

"I was listening just as Kropett was and I know your plan to double cross all of them, even your son. I intend to put a stop to this whole charade."

"It's one thing to issue idle threats, it's entirely different to follow through with them. You are not in a strong position to negotiate for your life."

"You can have my life. If I keep you from returning to the living realm it will be a trade I'm willing to make. At least if you're here you can't hurt anyone I love."

"Don't be so sure about that. Your grandfather has fought for this city longer than you have been alive. It would be a shame to send him, and every memory he holds dear, into the mist forever."

"You couldn't, you don't have that power."

"I would caution you not to, but you can test me if you want." Dungarvan paused waiting for Samuel to reply. When he didn't, he continued on. "I think it's time you rested."

Grabbing Samuel's face he pried open his mouth and forced him to drink the potion he had tricked him into drinking shortly after his arrival. Samuel gagged and tried to spit it out but the wizard clamped a firm hand over his nose and mouth.

"Swallow it."

Samuel resisted as long as he could before he needed to take a breath, finally succumbing to the wizard's demand and swallowing. It felt refreshing as it coated his parched throat, and if that was all it did he would have welcomed it without a fight. Unfortunately he knew the real purpose and there was no way to resist its effects, only just barely able to speak the word "Kurad" aloud, then his body went limp against the post.

The Ghosts of Pendar

CHAPTER THIRTY THREE

"I don't understand. How are you all here? Tell me you have not all died." Samuel asked, his breath still ragged. He stood flanked by Edward, Isabel, Kurad, and Relysis, within the castle gate the dwarves were still fighting to close against the push of Orgle's army led by the trolls.

"The wizard Dungarvan created a spell to bring us here. Well not us exactly, we can talk more after we get the gate closed."

The new arrivals joined the battle at the castle gate. Edward with his battleaxe, fighting side by side with his father, cleared a wide path for the rest of them to follow and push back against the gnomes. Kurad and Relysis led the miners into the fray just as Isabel provided a flurry of arrows to protect their flanks. Even with their help the battle raged through the night. In the end the gates were sealed, though at a great cost to Samuel's army.

"Come now, you promised an explanation of what has transpired," Samuel spoke once again to the reassembled team as he looked them all over. "I recognize you all, even though Edward you are much bigger than when I last saw you. However, I believe I need to be introduced to this skilled archer."

"Grandfather, I'm Isabel," she said as she stepped forward and offered a slight bow.

"Isabel, it is an honor to meet you," Samuel replied as he returned the bow. "I fear I have missed much."

"I know all about you." Isabel replied, impulsively stepping forward and wrapping her arms around the old king who quickly drew her in tighter. Isabel held on as long as she could, trying to fit a lifetime of missed hugs into one.

"I hate to break up this moment, but we do have much to cover," Edward interjected only to be immediately drawn into the embrace.

"It's been so long and you're grown now." Samuel's voice was hoarse when he finally released them both. Reaching over, he clasped Kurad by his shoulder, "You did a great job. There are no words I can say to convey that to you, and Relysis, as long as you're only here under this spell too, it's good to see you too."

"Likewise my friend. Did you know that I have now served under three Ellingstone kings?"

"Three?"

"I have a son named Samuel who sits on the throne. I chose to abdicate my crown to him due to injuries I suffered, he's the reason we are all here. Dungarvan abducted him and brought him into this realm, we are here to rescue him, so he can be brought back."

"That explains a lot of the increased activity and his reappearance alongside a new dragon."

"His son Rathlin, he shares the ability to change his identity to that of a dragon along with his own special skills."

Samuel appeared to consider this for a moment. "Come, I have someone else who Edward would very much like to meet."

Samuel led them through the remains of the castle, finally arriving in the great hall where Stephen sat alone at a table, apparently waiting for them to arrive.

"Stephen, you will not believe who has come to our rescue."

"I didn't believe the rumors swirling about the castle. Then you sent a runner to find me, and I dared only hope my nephew would recognize me after all this time."

"Of course, you have not changed since the last time I saw you."

"You were just a young boy, and now look at you. You would have nothing to fear from the Black Knight anymore."

Edward laughed at his uncle's reference to an old story that had been told to him time after time. "I was thankful when I was told that you all are only on loan to us here and won't be staying forever."

"Can I ask why you are still here and haven't gone on to the halls of Dagda?" Isabel asked after her introduction.

"Your grandfather and I, and all the soldiers protecting the castle, chose to stay here to protect the book. Until our duty is fulfilled we will not know our eternal rest."

"Is that where my grandmother is then, waiting?"

"Yes, she went ahead. There were too many reminders of the pain inflicted here with the defeat by Orgle and when Edward was missing."

"Let's get you caught up." Edward invited them all to sit at a large table.

The conversation took many twists and turns as they all sought to get Samuel up to speed on everything that had transpired in Pendar since his passing all the way up to the devastating defeat of the city of Pendar. It took many hours to cover all the victories and defeats, and only came to an end when Kurad interrupted.

"Samuel is in the city as we suspected. He just spoke my name, and it sounded as if he was close by."

"How is that you can hear him? I heard nothing."

"Since you appointed me to be Edward's protector I have shared a bond with whomever is king. Edward having passed it on to Samuel, now my bond is to him. In this realm it is enhanced, I can sometimes hear him when he speaks my name."

"Can you tell where he is specifically so we can go to him?" Isabel asked immediately.

"From the stories your father tells, your mother sounds like quite a woman, Isabel. You have that same tenacity."

"I guess so." Isabel had heard the tales of her mother when she was younger, though had a hard time connecting those to the mother she knew growing up. To Isabel her mom was nothing like the strong adventurous person in her father's tales.

"I can take Isabel and try to find him."

Isabel was yanked from her contemplation when Kurad suggested the two of them go together to find her brother, she almost fell off her chair when her father agreed.

"Isabel will be of great help, and from what I have seen she certainly won't slow you down. Find him and bring him back so you can take him home. The rest of us will plan our defense of the castle and this book Dungarvan is so intent upon stealing. I think we have to assume that the book and Samuel being here are related."

"Wait," Isabel stopped Kurad who was already several steps towards the door. "Father, we know Samuel has his sword with him, and already a few times it has reached across the gap between the world of the dead and living."

"Then we know without a doubt that these are all linked together. A magical weapon like that could shake the very foundations of this realm," Edward agreed.

"Isabel said it just now," Samuel said. "Dungarvan has come up with a plan to use my grandson, the tome of Pendar, and this magical sword to construct a pathway to return from the dead."

"You must hurry then," Stephen spoke up. "Tonight is the solstice, when the pathway is shortest between the realms."

The room exploded into activity after the quiet pronouncement faded away. Plans to protect the book accelerated along with the security around the castle, and orders for all available soldiers to report to the walls.

Isabel's head was spinning as she tried to take in everything that had just been revealed when a tap on her shoulder from Kurad reminded her they had maybe the most important task ahead of them. They had to save Samuel before the wizard could begin whatever ceremony he had planned to escape death himself. The very real possibility of it costing Samuel's life was not lost on her.

CHAPTER THIRTY FOUR

Isabel raced after Kurad who must have already heard enough to confirm in his mind what they needed to do. She didn't disagree it was just that, despite her father's endorsement, Kurad was much faster than she was, especially with a head start. However, several twists and turns within the confines of the castle had her reassessing their abilities as she gradually closed the gap he had initially garnered.

Her smaller stature lent itself to being much more nimble than her taller, heavier, counterpart. By the time they left the castle grounds over the wall they were back together, and when Kurad put up a hand to stop, they squatted down together. Isabel took a moment to catch her breath before she asked Kurad a question she had been pondering during their run.

"How accurate are Samuel's callings?"

"Nothing more than a vague suggestion."

"Yet, we're out here following his voice."

"Now that we are away from the castle, and we know the approximate direction, it will only be a matter of figuring out where Dungarvan would keep him."

"So we need to think like the wizard."

"Exactly. What would he be looking for as a base?"

"He would want it to be a safe distance from my grandfather's army."

"Yet, close enough to strike when he wanted to," Kurad countered.

"He has the dragons, so is there anywhere not close enough for him?"

"Good point. As you said, he has the dragons so that means he needs a very large area to take off from, and land.

Remember there are two of them, so it has to be even bigger. Can you think of a large plaza."

"That won't work for concealing Samuel."

"A warehouse," they spoke simultaneously. Isabel pinpointed where she felt they must be. "Just north of the district are a number of warehouses. The workers would stop in for an ale on the way home in any of the taverns in the area."

"Then let's go." Kurad paused when Isabel looked at him questioningly. "Lead on, you know your city better than I do. I will provide rear guard to your scout."

Isabel was taken by surprise, recovering quickly to give him a nod that she was ready. "Try to keep up." A thin smile creased his lips as she took off.

The streets were quiet with most of the gnome army still clustered in front of the castle gate and they were able to cover ground at a good pace. Still, Isabel didn't take unnecessary risks as she moved from cover to cover, which was plentiful along the rubble strewn streets. At times she was forced to backtrack when the route she wanted was blocked. Always, they sought the warehouses where they believed Dungarvan and Rathlin were holed up.

Time was limited though, and every impasse cost them more of the precious commodity. As minutes, then hours slipped away from the pair they were forced to take risks, each one bigger than the last until they pushed their luck too far. It came as they felt they were finally nearing their goal, then suddenly the tables turned and they were no longer the searchers, but became the ones sought.

There was no warning as the pair crossed the exposed intersection other than the sound of rushing wind from the beast flying low overhead.

"Kurad, run!" The time for even pretending to be stealthy was gone as the dragon bore down on the pair. A large plume of flames chased them as they dove through an open doorway into the hollowed out Darkwood Tavern.

"Are you okay?" Kurad asked, flames licking at the doorframe dissipated slowly into the mist.

"I got careless, I'm so sorry."

"It's not your fault. If there were a true sun in this realm it would be well beyond its highest point in the sky. I'm just as aware as you are that we are short on time."

Another blast from the dragon shook the remnants of the tavern and had them both looking for a way out.

"We have to be close. The dragons have stayed well away from the castle during this last battle. I have to assume it's to protect their prized possession."

"Which way out of here? We need to get to their lair."

"You want me to continue to lead? I got us into this mess."

"We're both alive because of your warning."

"Follow me, there has to be a way out the back."

Isabel resumed the lead, clambering over roof beams, tables, and chairs that had been tossed about, the two racing to get out of the building. It was not a moment too soon that they emerged into the alley. The dragon landed on top of the Darkwood and flattened the remainder of the building just as they cleared it. Isabel gave a quick backwards glance to see if the dragon had spotted them, but couldn't be sure before they darted around the next corner.

She tried to stick to the darkest shadows as she led Kurad towards the warehouse district. There were no explosions of flame around them so she could only hope they had lost the dragon, that he searched for them in the rubble of the tavern. They weren't that lucky.

The building came crashing down right in front of her when the dragon swooped down out of the sky. Fortunately for them when he landed on top of the building it collapsed beneath him and he was caught up in the wave of cascading granite blocks. Kurad grabbed Isabel from behind as she skidded to a halt, the ground shaking beneath them. They only had moments before the dragon could get clear of the avalanche and they needed to make the most of the opportunity.

Kurad took the lead as they got their feet under them and raced away through the nearest open door he could find. They were too exposed on the street and no matter what they found in the building would most certainly be better than what they were leaving behind. They couldn't have been more wrong.

Going down in a heap in front of her, Kurad's legs were taken out from under him by some unseen foe that lay in wait. Isabel barely escaped the same fate by a troll's spear only because Kurad had knocked it from the beast's hands in his fall. Dipping sideways, she saw the troll come lumbering out from the shadows and tackle Kurad as he tried to regain his feet.

Isabel reached for her bow, notched an arrow, and drew it back. Just as she was about to fire, the vast room they were in was suddenly illuminated. The light was blinding even in the ever present haze of this realm and she had to throw a hand up before her eyes so she didn't lose her sight, her shot flying wide of any target she had been sighted on.

"Put the bow away or your friend will not survive to return to his body back amongst the living. You really don't want to witness a troll tearing someone in half," Dungarvan stated, letting the light he held aloft fade away.

Isabel eased her hand down from her eyes to see the wizard standing across from her. She didn't, however, drop her bow. Instead she reached back and pulled two arrows from her quiver.

"You must be Dungarvan, I had been told you were clever. I'm not so sure. Do you think I couldn't shoot you both before your lumbering creature could even formulate the thought required to carry out your demands?" To emphasis her point, in the blink of an eye she notched one arrow and had it at full draw, trained on the troll's face, a tight shot from where Kurad was being held. She kept the other in her hand ready to reload in an instant.

"The troll will require more than one arrow to send into the mist, there is no way you can save him and your brother." The wizard yanked a chain she hadn't seen till it pulled tight. It brought Samuel staggering forward from where he was hidden behind the wizard's cloak.

"Samuel!" Isabel screamed, shifting her aim to the wizard.

"He's not all here at the moment so he likely won't recognize you."

"What did you do to him? If you hurt him…"

"He was misbehaving, it's only a spell to make him more compliant."

"Reverse it now or you will feel the bite of dwarven steel."

"You have a decision to make. Whose life will you attempt to save?"

"Isabel, get out of here," Kurad pleaded with her even as he was squeezed tighter in the troll's embrace.

A boot scuffing the floor behind her made the decision for her. Twirling about she sent the arrow directly towards Rathlin who stood blocking the doorway. Somehow the shot was knocked away as he desperately whipped his sword across his body, however, the second arrow struck true and he staggered away to collapse onto the floor clutching his injured side.

Isabel only had a moment to get clear of the building, dashing out into the haze. Samuel had Kurad with him, she doubted Dungarvan would waste another bargaining chip and harm him, so all she could do was get back to the castle in time to assist in stopping Dungarvan in securing the book for the ceremony that was only hours away. Isabel wasn't sure she would make it in time, if at all, but she meant to do whatever she could to be there when her brother needed her.

"Why did you allow her to shoot you?" Dungarvan snapped at Rathlin as he lay writhing on the floor.

"There was no way I thought she could get off a second shot that fast."

"Are you going to be able to fly? We need to leave here shortly to finish off Samuel's army. Orgle's stunt was nothing more than to soften them up. Now is the time to finish this."

CHAPTER THIRTY FIVE

"How do the defenses look, General?" Samuel asked as they stood atop the castle walls and surveyed the battle positions below.

""You've learned a lot since we last fought together."

"It's been a lifetime of battles, more when I stop and think about it, though I try not to. Do you realize not a week has gone by without the gnomes trying to chase us from this castle?"

"For all their faults they are tenacious."

"If it weren't for the trolls we would have never given up the city all those years ago."

"Bah, don't get me started, me King. I've had many occasions to consider how different Pendar's history would be if not for that day when we lost you."

"You have my namesake to lead Pendar now, and I'm sure Edward will continue to offer his guidance."

"Maybe it isn't my place to say, but as your general I'll take my liberties. Edward isn't coming home with us. He was actually assassinated by one of Dungarvan's men. Isabel doesn't know so we're keeping it quiet until we rescue her brother."

"I need to talk to him." Samuel didn't wait for the general to say anymore, instead rushing off to locate his son. He knew Edward was supposed to be setting up the defense of the book so he immediately went to the library. Standing at the doorway for a moment, he looked at his boy with newfound sorrow.

"Hey, I didn't see you there. Why don't we move it to the crypt? It would be much more defensible." Edward paused, looking at his father. "What's wrong?"

"Relysis told me the truth of how you came to be here."

"I'm sorry I didn't tell you. We were trying to keep it from Isabel."

"He told me that too. Don't be sorry, tell me how you are handling it. Do you have any questions?"

"I don't think it's really sunk in yet. I've been trying to soak up every moment with Isabel, and I can't wait to see Samuel again. However, I know that once we're done here and defeat the dragons they are going home without me."

"You're confident we will win."

"I've defeated him before, I intend to do it again."

"There are two now, how do you overcome that?"

"I will have help this time I didn't before, right?"

"It's been amazing to meet Isabel, and I'm sure Samuel will be equally impressive, but we need to send them both back home. Whatever it takes, count me in." Samuel pulled Edward into his embrace, attempting to process the knowledge of the death of his son. It hadn't last nearly long enough when Edward spoke up.

"You never answered me about why we don't move it to the crypt."

"We've tried," Samuel said, wiping away a tear, "It seems that it's anchored here. Maybe because this is where it is back in your realm. Sorry, I mean, you know what I mean."

"We'll deal with it from here then."

"So you have a plan?"

Horns from men on the walls echoed across the castle grounds as they called the army of Pendar to defend the castle one more time.

"I guess we'll figure it out. Let's go see what we have going on outside." Just like the other defenders the two former kings of Pendar rushed off to answer the call. Edward stopped short of the wall, his father asking him to stay out of sight as he went out onto the wall.

The scene before him was just as Samuel had seen many times before with one, make that two, giant exceptions. Dragons, a pair of them stood at the front of the army of ghosts, and upon closer inspection at their feet were a pair of trolls each securing a prisoner. Kurad was easily identifiable, which meant the other was his grandson.

"You've come to return Samuel and Kurad, that was very kind of you. Release them now and I will have my men open the gates for them."

One dragon's laughter shook the ground beneath them, clearly this was Dungarven. The fact that he thought Samuel's remark ridiculous evidenced his arrogance.

"You know what I need. The question is whether you will give it over freely, or will I be forced to tear every remaining block of this castle down before I take it from you?"

"I gave you my terms. Anything less and my army will be forced to take them from you."

"You gave no such thing, you want me to just let them go without any compensation."

"Then we agree. Release them now," he shouted across to the dragons before turning to Edward. "Lead the dwarves out to kill the trolls, when they disappear into the mist Samuel and Kurad will be free. You have to do it before the dragons realize what we are doing and react."

Edward slipped off the wall to carry out his mission while Samuel stayed atop the wall to distract the dragons.

"What is your answer, Dungarvan?"

"I will not even humor you with a response," the dragon's voice boomed back over the space between them. "I have brought my son with me. You may recognize him, he was the one who destroyed Pendar. He's here to finish what he started." The wizard gave Rathlin a nod of his giant head and the younger dragon proceeded to spread his wings and launch himself into the air.

Samuel felt in that moment his gamble wasn't going to work. Edward and the dwarves came rushing out from the gate towards the trolls flanking the lone dragon. The beast taking flight saw them and was making the adjustment to breathe death from above down upon them when a small figure ran out onto the plaza with a bow in her hand. "Isabel."

Arrow after arrow streaked skyward, every one of them focused on the blood stain Samuel could see on the airborne dragon's side. Somehow Isabel knew of its injury and her arrows flew true, striking him time after time in that same spot while he screamed in rage trying desperately to twist away from the steel tipped missiles. Then, before all who witnessed the onslaught in amazement, the beast suddenly dissipated and faded into the mist.

Dungarvan roared in rage at the loss of the other beast and turned his own flames to the dwarves still charging across the plaza. Shields were raised immediately and their rush ground to a halt, flames washing over the dwarves hiding under the protection of their sturdy steel shields.

"You will not save your son this time!" Dungarvan roared as the flames dissipated.

The dwarves moved forward again with Edward at the forefront. Dungarvan quickly grabbed the troll holding young Samuel, ripping the king away before tossing the troll aside.

Watching from the wall, Samuel knew exactly what Dungarvan meant to do now. Leaving the scene of the battle below he raced from the wall, leaping over granite blocks as he sought to reach the book before the dragon did. The hour of the solstice was growing near and that was all that the wizard needed to complete his ceremony.

He was nearly to the library when the castle shook under his feet so hard he was upended and sent tumbling. Picking himself up even as blocks continued to rain down around him, he pushed forward knowing the dragon most surely had landed squarely on the castle above the library.

Rounding the corner the view before his was just as he thought. The castle had been flattened and the dragon was digging frantically through the rubble to secure the book.

"The book isn't there, we moved it," Samuel lied to the beast.

"Save your false words, I can smell the old leather is near even now."

"Give me the boy and you can have the book without a fight."

"I'm not concerned with a mere human. What can you do to me?"

"You weren't happy to see me, I thought you might have recalled our last encounter." Edward stepped into the room and through the dust that still hung in the air. His breathing was heavy from his exertions. "Take me instead of my son for whatever you have planned."

"It is tempting, but it is his magic in the sword that I need to create the pathway back to the living. Besides, his body will be a much better host than your old worn out one."

"If I put an arrow through him right now he will be of no use to you and his magic will die with him." Isabel emerged from behind her father. "He would find it a better option than to let you return to the living in his body. I would ask him, but he looks like you have put a spell on him."

"It is time for you all to go," Dungarvan said, pulling the book from the rubble. His prize found, he immediately took a deep breath that sent them all diving behind a large block of stone before he released a fireball that exploded where they had all been standing.

"We have to stop him," Samuel said as he helped Isabel back to her feet.

"He will need to revert back to his wizard form if he's going to go back as Samuel. Do we wait until then?" Edward asked as he crawled over to where the other two huddled.

"Regardless, that is moments away. Midnight is nearly upon us, we have to act now."

"Isabel is right, we can't wait."

Peering around their protective barrier, they could see they were right. Dungarvan had released the dragon spell and was positioning the book on a makeshift table. Going over to Samuel he forced the groggy young king to grip the sword, guiding him as he drew it out. The magic responded to his touch and sent out a pulse of blue light that shook the entire castle and left Dungarvan struggling to keep his feet under him.

As soon as the ground stopped shaking he got back to his task, the hour finally arrived for his ceremony and anticipated release from death's grip. The three watching saw their chance when Dungarvan raised the blade above the book, ready to plunge it deep into the cover and activate the spell within.

Edward was already moving with his battleaxe raised even as Isabel drew back her bow to find a clear shot at the wizard. It was then, out of nowhere, a form streaked by them all and threw himself onto the wizard. The magical blade with its blue arcs racing up and down the blade missed the book only to be buried deep into the chest of Dungarvan.

The next few seconds seemed to stretch slowly as the realization of what just happened registered on the wizard's face. His eyes rested on the crumpled form of Kropett who lay on top of the book looking up at him.

"You never deserved to go back." The gnome's words were forced through clenched teeth.

As soon as the little gnome spoke his judgment the magic of Samuel's sword exploded out through the wizard and coursed through the entire city of Pendar. Blue magic searching out and striking down every member of his army, sending them beyond the mist to never reform again before the power collapsed back upon itself into the blade in one last flash of light and tremor.

"I couldn't let him do it," Kropett said as he pulled himself up to sit upon the book.

"The magic spared you." Edward came forward.

"I guess I redeemed myself in the end?"

"You did," young Samuel said as he shook off the last effects of the wizard's spell. "You saved my life."

CHAPTER THIRTY SIX

Isabel arrived back at the castle at Kurad's side, the pair having made a sweep of the city to make sure the sword's power hadn't left any of the wizard's army behind. She led them immediately to her father, grandfather, and brother to report their findings.

"I'm glad to report to all three kings of Pendar that we're all clear, there is not a single ghost from Dungarvan's army left within the city."

"Then it seems your work here is done."

"Are you trying to get rid of us, Grandfather? I thought you would at least want my father to stay longer."

"There's something I need to tell you Isabel, you too Samuel." Edward motioned for the pair to come sit with him, taking a deep breath before he spoke his next words. "I'm not going home with you two."

"What to do you mean, Father? We came here because of the spell, I'm actually surprised we didn't automatically go back as soon as Dungarvan was destroyed," Samuel stated.

"You knew this whole time." Isabel frowned, her lip trembling as she began to put several clues together.

"I did. I'm not here because of the same spell that brought the rest of you here. There was an assassin who was waiting for me in Relysis's quarters." Edward pulled out the dragon claw amulet and laid it on the table.

"Father, no!" Isabel screamed, jumping up to ran to him. "It can't be true, you have to come home with us. I don't know what I will do without you."

"It's true, there isn't anything I can do to change it. I need you to promise you will take care of your mother. She already knows my fate, that is why you need to get back there as fast as you can. I will be with my father. We're all going to the halls of Dagda, all the ghosts of Pendar are going home. Their final battle has been won."

Long moments passed before anyone spoke again, it was Samuel who finally broke the silence. "Father, you've done all you could to get us ready to lead our people. I promise Mother will never be alone, the entire city of Drogheda will be there for her. We will be together again someday, when each of our times has passed."

Grateful for their brief time together, they knew it was time to go. More tears were shed as goodbyes were shared amongst all those returning to Drogheda and the last of those who were going to the halls of their ancestors.

"I hope you can forgive me for not telling you sooner. I wanted our last adventure together to be special, and not tainted."

"Don't worry I forgive you, I could never hold that against you. I love you, Father, and I will miss you fiercely." Isabel squeezed him tight one last time, tears flowing freely knowing it was the last time for many years to come.

"Give your Mother a hug for me, just like this one." The embrace lasted long between the two, even longer when her brother joined in. Kurad finally came to Edward's rescue and announced they must go.

"Come now, our bodies have been empty for too long already. I'm not ready to stay here just yet."

"I second that, I could use an ale to soothe my throat," Relysis said as he wiped a tear from his own eyes.

"One last question, what happened to Kropett?" Isabel asked as they were shouldering their gear.

"He's been invited to join us in the hall as a hero of Pendar. I believe he is going to accept," Samuel said as he too gave his grandchildren a hug before sending them on their way.

It was a long journey for the four of them, but at long last they found themselves back in Drogheda. Walking through the quiet halls they arrived in the hospital ward. Each went to their respective bodies and looked about, the four of them shared one last look between them. It had been an adventure like no other any had experienced, but now it was over and the last step seemed to be the most nerve wracking.

Unsure of what to do they watched Kurad lie down on his prone form, seeing his spirit merge back into his body. Each in turn followed suit. Isabel waited for the others to take their turns to make sure they all came through okay.

Waking up coughing, she pushed herself to an elbow to look around the room and make sure they were all back before she laid back heavily on the table. Calls went out around them and healers were suddenly rushing about tending to their returned patients. Isabel closed her eyes against the tears as relief flooded through her body, only opening them when a soft voice reached her.

"I knew your father would make sure you came back to me."

"He did, Mother." Isabel looked up with a gentle smile. "You won't believe it, but I met my grandfather too."

"I want to hear all about it from you and Samuel."

"You will," Isabel promised, closing her eyes against the pain of realizing her father wasn't going to be there when she opened them again.

The whole of it all felt like a wild dream. The only proof she had that it wasn't was the dragon claw amulet she clutched in her hand. Even though it was from the assassin who had taken her father from her, it was a final memento from their last adventure together and if he was okay with where he was then she needed to be too.

She knew it was going to take her a while to get to that same place, but she also knew she had time and more adventures in her future. Stories she would get to share with him some day when they met again. A slight grin creased her lips at that beautiful thought.

The Ghosts of Pendar

Mayor Tralee pushed his way into the room through the throng who had gathered outside upon hearing the news of their awakening. He needed to see for himself that all four of them had really returned safely to Drogheda. Seeing that they were all awake and talking came as a great relief. He had gone through the same process and knew they too would emerge unscathed, if not profoundly changed, from the experience just as he had.

Smiling to himself for his part in bringing them home, he turned and went back out into the hall in the direction of his office. There was work to be done and he knew there would be time to share their stories later.

THE END

ABOUT THE AUTHOR

It was a lot of fun writing another Pendar book this year. The creative process is just so much fun. Even though balancing family, work, writing, and trying to keep active with cycling can be trying sometimes it's worth the extra effort.

I'm blessed with a daughter who has grown up to be a wonderful young lady, and a great model for my strong female characters, and a teenage son in baseball so my wife and I are busy just trying to keep up with them. In spite, or maybe because, of our busy schedule we've added a travel trailer into the mix so we can get out and see the country together. We've even used it for a couple of weekend festival book signing events and I can't wait to do more of those when I'm able to forego the day job and pursue my passion full time.

Thanks for taking the time to let me tell you about myself.

Made in the USA
Columbia, SC
20 May 2022

60692885R00136